Remarkable Dorcas Armstrong Holt Buchanan

By

Dee Armstrong Crabtree

Dedication

Dedicated to the innumerable descendants of Dorcas Armstrong Holt Buchanan.

Copyright

Copyright 2020
All Rights
Dee Armstrong Crabtree
ISBN: 9781660799664

Special Thanks

I owe special thanks to several people and organizations. For their help, I am deeply grateful to Ryan Bender and Nik Schreiner for their editing services. I would also like to thank the staff of the Mifflin County Historical Society, as well as staff of the Cumberland County Historical Society.

About the Author

A lifelong Hoosier, Dee Armstrong Crabtree studied journalism at Saint Mary-of-the-Woods College and has been published in various local, regional and national publications. In addition to writing feature articles for several publications, Ms. Crabtree is the author of four non-fiction books and three novels.

Other Books by this Author

A Simply Wonderful Life

Simply Wonderful Holidays

Simply Wonderful Travels

Records Retention Made Simple

Simply Wonderful Sailing

Promise Road

Uncle Imblay's Fortune

Introduction

This novel is based on the life of Dorcas Armstrong Holt Buchanan, reportedly the first white woman settler of Mifflin County, Pennsylvania. There are so many conflicting stories about Dorcas that it is difficult to know what is true and what is exaggeration, or perhaps even mere speculation. Even her obituary seems somewhat contradictory to other stories and documents related to her life. As you read, please keep in mind that this is a work of fiction, based on the stories that have been told about her for over 200 years.

Some facts of her life, like her ownership of the land, are well-documented. Arthur Buchanan, Jr.'s letters are on record with the Pennsylvania Archives and Arthur, Sr.'s petition to the Carlisle Quarter Sessions Court is on record, as well. The elder Buchanan's estate papers are also on file with the Cumberland County Historical Society.

The names of the Holt and Buchanan children are likewise documented among the legal archives of the areas where they once lived. I've used their real names and, along with the names of some of Dorcas's grandchildren. As is true in many families, many of the same first names were used repeatedly throughout multiple generations. There were at least three Arthurs and three Janes in the Armstrong and Buchanan lines. For this reason, I've inserted an abbreviated family tree for reference at the end of the book to help you, should you get lost along the way.

Most of the battles and attacks that you will read about in this book, perpetrated by both the Native American tribes and the European colonists, are taken from recorded history. The rest of the stories regarding the many feats and accomplishments of the Armstrong Holt Buchanan family are a combination of history and folklore.

I believe that I've portrayed Dorcas as she truly must have been because I have lived with several of her descendants who perpetuate her spirit just as much as they do her bloodline. Regardless of whether any of the stories of her bold actions are fact or fiction, the reports of the type of woman she was have a strong ring of truth to my ears. As I mentioned above, I witnessed that same great spirit in my great-grandmother when I was a child and I always marveled at it, wondering where the heck that uncommon independence, strength and courage came from, especially in that day and age. There is a centuries-old adage that you can't beat out what is bred in. Apparently, you can't beat out an indominable pioneering spirit like that of Dorcas Armstrong Holt Buchanan. I see it alive and well now in my mother, my sister, my daughter and my granddaughter.

Whether any of the folklore surrounding Dorcas' life is based in fact can never really be known for sure. However, her incredible spirit lives on in many of her countless direct descendants to this very day. I suspect that it will exist in her descendants for many years to come. That amazing spirit cannot be beaten out. It will not die.

The grave of Dorcas Buchanan

Lewistown, Pennsylvania

Chapter One

May 1755

It was a pleasant, peaceful morning along Kishacoquillas Creek, a small stream winding through the wilds of Pennsylvania and feeding into the wide Juniata River. The only sounds that filled the air were that of creek water running over the rocks and the murmur of bees flitting about a nearby patch of honeysuckle. Bright sunlight filtered through the trees and the warm breeze carried a hint of the summer that was soon to be.

Horace Watson had been standing creek-side since dawn, dangling a line in hopes of catching a sizeable bronzeback. He was bored and impatient with his lack of success thus far. He'd planned to catch something decent early in the day, take it home and fry himself up a nice breakfast. If his catch was big enough, he could eat all day on one fish. After all, there was no one on his homestead to feed but old Horace himself. His wife, Miranda, had succumbed to the fever the previous winter. His family had questioned the wisdom of their migrating west at their ages, both of them 64 years old at the time. Now Horace himself was beginning to question it himself.

Horace scratched his scraggly, sandy beard while considering his options. He was about to put down his rod in favor of a short walk downstream to Arthur Buchanan's tavern for a faster, easier breakfast, when he heard Kilkenny, the Buchanans' scruffy mutt, filling the valley with his raucous barks. Horace turned downstream in the direction of the commotion just in time to see Buchanan's wife, Dorcas, running full-bore toward the creek. He watched in astonishment as both woman and dog leapt without hesitation into the cold, rushing water. A bend in the creek obstructed part of the view of the scene, so he dropped his fishing pole and trotted downstream a few yards to see what the uproar was all about.

He rounded the bend just in time to see Dorcas Buchanan, now waist-deep in the stream, grab the antler of a massive buck with her left hand and pull herself astride the creature as though she were mounting a horse for a leisurely ride. This would be a ride for sure, but most definitely not a leisurely one.

The sprightly Mrs. Buchanan was a legendary huntress of deer who used unconventional methods to bring down her prey. Horace had heard many a tale of how she and her dog would chase deer into the water to drown them. He had seen several stag racks hanging as evidence over her bake oven, including one at the center of the wall that reportedly came from a 1000-pound buck. Given that the antlers spread well over five feet from tip to tip, Horace was inclined to believe the story. He had not yet witnessed this magnificent feat in person but he now found himself staring and gaping at the amazing spectacle in complete awe.

"Oh, Dorkey! Be careful there, girl," yelled Horace.

As Horace counseled Dorcas from the shoreline, her husband ambled out of the tavern, flanked by three regular customers from *The Bounding Elk*. His step-sons, Henry and Thomas, dark haired, dark eyed copies of each other, left the field they were tilling to watch the sport. A girl of about ten, a miniature version of Dorcas, and a six-year-old boy who appeared to be of the same stock, pushed through the crowd of men to watch their mother. Sons Arthur, Jr. and William, both very close replicas of their strong-jawed, ruddy, Scotch-Irish father, were just returning from a morning hunting trip and they joined the crowd to take in the show. They never tired of watching their feisty mother succeed in what other women wouldn't even dream of trying to do.

Horace was shocked that the men all stood along shore cheering Dorcas on but not a one of them stepped forward to aid her in her battle with the enormous creature. It surely weighed at least ten times what she did and he feared for her safety.

"Get him, Dorkey. You can do it," Arthur exclaimed, chewing on his pipe and grinning widely. He appeared to be greatly amused by his wife's efforts and was in no rush to jump in and help her.

"Arthur," cried out an incredulous Horace, "Aren't you going to get out there and give your wife a hand with that thing?"

"No sir," he answered with a confident smile. "She's done this plenty of times before and she knows what she's doing. She doesn't like me to step in. This is her game." Horace shook his befuddled head. *A game*, he called it. She might be taller and stronger than many women, but Horace couldn't help but wonder how much strength was in those long limbs, given that she was so thin. She could be seriously injured or even killed.

The men and children watched, cheering Dorcas on as she got a firm grip on the deer's rack with both hands, then twisted and pushed his head under the water. The battle began in earnest as the startled animal appeared to suddenly realize that his life was in danger at the hands of this small creature sitting astride his back.

As the two fought, the neat and tidy tavern mistress began to dissolve and she was swiftly replaced by a wild, fearless warrior. Her long, cinnamon hair fell away from its pinning, while the shoulder stitching of her blue cotton dress shredded. Her white cap had already floated downstream, far beyond rescuing.

Dorcas paid no mind whatsoever to her appearance or to her audience. Her thoughts were now focused on killing this deer that might well feed her family and others for several months to come. Doing so commanded complete concentration and every bit of passion and strength that she could muster.

The great beast's feet stirred the creek bed beneath the pair of adversaries, turning the water muddy brown. The thrashing of the huntress above agitated the surface of the creek so violently that onlookers could see only a jumble of splashing water, a flying linen skirt and the tan haunches of the buck trying to throw off his assailant. Both of the strong, determined foes wrestled and writhed excitedly until the buck could stand no more. Unable to endure, the defeated creature finally collapsed into the peace of the creek.

The assembled throng applauded Dorcas as she dragged her prize by his rack toward the creek bank. Once she reached the shallows where the buoyancy of the water no longer aided her efforts, the men waded into the water to help her bring her quarry onto dry land. Once ashore, Dorcas was heartily congratulated as the men admired the size of the slain animal.

"Dorcas," Horace questioned as the excitement died down, "Wouldn't it be easier to just shoot him?"

"Easier, yes," she answered as she wrung out her skirts. "But, to my mind, shooting animals taints the meat. My way is cleaner. And I think it is more humane, as well. Shooting doesn't always kill the pour souls quick-like, but they never linger when they drown. They go the instant that the water fills their lungs."

"It looks like you're taking life in your own hands with this business. Did you ever get hurt by one of those things?"

"No. Not yet, anyway. My pa taught me how to do it this way. He used to do it all the time before he got too old to run and chase them. It might look like they are fighting strong, but once they get in deep enough water, they can't really put up much of a fight."

"I think this fellow is your biggest one to date," noted Arthur. "We'll be able to fill the smokehouse right up with this."

"I'll leave that all to you. I don't know what you aimed to do today but you and the boys best be getting on this," she said, pointing to the deer. "I am going to go in and put on a dry dress. I'm soaked to the bone and my dress sleeve is about to fall clean off."

The men turned and watched with admiration as the victorious huntress sauntered up to the house as serene and calm as if she was returning from a church meeting. Her wet, shredded dress and her fallen hairdo were the only remnants of battle that remained about her person.

"Buchanan, that's quite a spirited woman you got there," exclaimed one of the customers from the tavern.

"I do love that woman's wild spirit," he answered. "It's what first drew me to her. Did you ever hear the story of how I met her?"

"No, but I'd like to hear it now, if you don't mind," exclaimed Horace. He knew Dorcas as a kind, welcoming tavern mistress and a good neighbor. After the battle he just witnessed, he wanted to learn everything that he could.

"If I don't mind? It's one of my favorite stories and I never tire of telling it. She was the Widow Holt in those days," he began. His gray eyes glimmered with amusement as a wry grin slowly crossed his tan, creased face.

"I'd just come back to Lancaster after riding posse with Sheriff Smith and I stopped in for some grub at the place down the street from the new courthouse they'd just built. I was sitting there talking to a bunch of fellas when the door burst open and in stormed this wild-eyed young woman just a huffing and puffing and caring a big old stick. She looked around the room and saw the man she was looking for and, just bold as you please, grabbed him by the ear and pulled him backwards till his chair fell clean over. He had no choice but to go outside with her cause she was half dragging him. Once she got him out on the street, she started thumping on him. She beat on him again and again until the sheriff came along and pulled her off the poor soul."

"What? That sweet, pretty lady there attacked a man? Why in the world would she do that," asked one of the tavern regulars.

"She sure did," Arthur chuckled. "Seems he was married to her dearest friend, Clarissa. The scoundrel beat up Clarissa pretty bad, left her black and blue all over. When Dorcas got wind of it, she went plumb crazy. She wasn't about to let some man get away with hurting one of her women friends like that."

Arthur's audience chuckled in amazement as much as amusement. He loved nothing more than to entertain an audience with a good story and this particular one always shocked and delighted every soul who heard it.

"The judge just so happened to be at the courthouse that day, so Sheriff Smith took her directly in to see him. When she dragged that poor man outside, we all followed to watch what was happening and then we all followed when the sheriff led her off. Her dress was all amess and her hair was falling down, kind of like she looked just a minute ago. She wasn't soaking wet that day but she was a big old mess, just the same. And she had a fire in her eye that scared nearly everyone in the courthouse."

"I could see Dorcas doing that. She's not afraid of anybody or anything," remarked one of the tavern customers. "Surely the judge didn't lock her up for that, did he?"

"Nah., I think that the sheriff just hauled her in to get her to stop beating on the fellow and to let him make a getaway. She was cocky and wouldn't apologize for what she did. She even got sassy with the old judge himself. But he just scolded her, then told her to go home and to not do it again."

"That woman would fight the devil himself if she saw fit," remarked someone from the back of the crowd.

"She would at that, if she thought she could right some egregious wrong. She's a real right-fighter. If she thought someone was whooping an innocent dog, she'd turn around and whoop the tar out of the fella doing it."

"She certainly would," murmured her oldest son, Henry.

"I fell in love with her right then and there in front of that judge. She has showed herself to have an incredible sense of right and wrong, how she put herself in harm's way to help a friend. There's a fierceness and fire in her that I never ever saw in any other soul on this earth, man or woman. I married that woman the moment that I was able to prove to her that I was worthy of being her husband."

Chapter Two

In the years leading up to the summer of 1754, the Buchanans had been living a quiet, modest life in Carlisle. They'd helped Arthur's brother William run a tavern there, while Arthur continued trapping and trading furs. In July of that year, the Albany Purchase was completed, opening up more land for sale to new settlers. Arthur suspected that a sea of ambitious pioneers would soon flood the roads leading west and he intended to make a hearty profit from the traffic that would be flowing into the valley. Come August, the ambitious, young couple loaded everyone that they loved, along with enough things to start a new household, into three wagons. They headed out over the Blue Ridge Mountains, eager to be the first in line to capitalize on the vast opportunities Kishacoquillas Valley might offer.

Arthur Buchanan had spent several years exploring the hills and dales of Pennsylvania during his trapping expeditions, and he knew exactly where he wanted to settle. During his early years as a fur trader, he'd made a good friend in Chief Kishacoquillas who lived in Ohesson, an Indian village, about a three-day ride northwest of Carlisle. Ohesson, a small community of about

100 souls, consisted of several rows of birchbark wigwams belonging to members of different but closely related tribes; the Shawnee, the Susquehannock, the Lenape and the Iroquois.

Buchanan was a shrewd businessman. It was obvious to him that this area, where the Kishacoquillas Creek poured into the Juniata, would be a prime spot for a trading post. The natives of Ohesson were peaceful and friendly, and their settlement sat smack-dab in the middle of a convenient intersection of the north-south and east-west routes through the mountains. Anyone coming through this part of the wilderness would travel through this intersection at one time or another. He was convinced that the possibilities for a prosperous life were endless if he could buy a parcel of land and settle his family in this special spot.

As soon as Arthur had put his family and his wagons a respectful distance from the village, he called on Chief Kishacoquillas to ask for his blessing to stay on property closer to the village. He'd lived near and among these tribes long enough to know that they valued respect and good manners as much as any refined English Lord and he always treated them accordingly. He found his long-time friend sitting by the in front of his hut, fashioning some small thing from wood with his knife.

"Buchanan, good to see you my old friend," exclaimed Kishacoquillas as he looked up from his work spotted Buchanan walking toward him. The old chief treasured his friendship with this inimitable white man. Arthur spoke the Shawnee language but Kishacoquillas' mastery of the English language far outshone Arthur's rudimentary Shawnee, so the two almost always conversed in English. Kishacoquillas appreciated Arthur's attempts at speaking Shawnee but those attempts were so far off the mark that it was just easier to speak English.

"And it is good to see you. I trust that you and your family are all doing well."

"My family is faring quite well. And yours?"

"Me and my kin are all in good health. Matter of fact, I brought them with me."

"Where are they," Chief Kish asked, looking around to see them.

"Just around the bend a bit."

"Why do they wait there?"

"Because I wouldn't dream of bringing my family here without a proper invitation from you. We come hoping to make an extended visit of it.

You see, we want to stay a little while and maybe do some business with your people."

"Go. Bring them now. Your people are always welcome here. Will you lodge with me?"

"Oh no. I think you for the kind offer but there are too many of us and I wouldn't want to impose. I brought my wife and all of our children. We have our wagons and some tents for shelter. Would it be alright with you if we set up a small camp at the downstream end of the village? We don't want to be any trouble to you or to your people."

"Buchanan, go bring them now. You'll set up here near me," Kish ordered, pointing to a smooth, flat clearing not far from the edge of the creek.

Arthur followed the orders that he had hoped and prayed would be issued. Dorcas and the family were sitting in the wagons, waiting patiently, when he returned.

"Alright. Let's move the wagons. The chief gave us permission to set up camp right next to his place." Dorcas sighed with relief. Her husband hadn't mentioned any sort of alternate plan had his original one failed. She had worried that if things didn't work out, that they would have to turn around and go right back to Carlisle. They were all extremely road weary from the trip and she wanted to set up camp as soon as possible so that they could have a decent meal and a good night's sleep.

"Now you all listen to me carefully," he cautioned. "These folks who are now our hosts are civilized people who deserve our respect, no matter what you might have heard folks in town say about Indians. You treat them right and mind your manners, just like you would folks in town. You stay in our camp and don't go aimlessly wandering around their homes and property. You be polite to everyone you meet."

"Arthur Buchanan, just who do you think you're talking to? We've raised these children right and you know that they will do you proud."

"I know that but it's very important that they don't forget their raising, especially the youngsters, if we aim to live here. We can't have them running around and forgetting the way that they should behave around civilized folk."

"They'll be alright. We'll all watch out for each other. Don't let that worry you none at all."

The Buchanans rolled their wagons into Ohesson and the residents all came out to greet them, curious about this white family that chose to come stay in their village. They'd had white men visitors before, but never a white woman and her children. Arthur and Dorcas set up a temporary camp a few yards from his friend's home, exactly where they were directed, careful not to let their clan spread out too much. They were conscientious about not overstepping their bounds.

The welcome they receive was a warm one. The small village took on a festive atmosphere that evening as the women of the tribe invited the family to share in their evening meals and Dorcas shared the food that she was preparing, as well. The visitors and their hosts all soon relaxed in each other's company.

When the families had finished their suppers and the women were putting the children to bed, Chief Kishacoquillas invited Arthur to come sit by his fire for a quiet, late-night talk. It had been quite a while since Buchanan had visited the man he referred to as Kish, and both men were eager to rekindle their friendship and catch up on what had been going on in each other's lives.

They sat crossed legged on the floor of the chief's home, sharing a pipe. These two had spent countless hours sitting just like this, back in the day when Buchanan was a fur trader who asked nothing of Kishacoquillas but his good company. They talked at length of wives and children, of weather and game, of forts being built and villages being moved. Eventually, Arthur felt comfortable enough to share his long-range plans with his trusted friend.

"Kishacoquillas, can you tell me who owns that nice little clearing across the way?" Buchanan was eyeing the spot on the west side of the creek, directly across from the council house of the Indians. The council-house sat to the south of the village, leaving the piece of property that Buchanan wanted convenient to but out of sight of the homes. It was a prime parcel on a small rise between the creek and the heavily traveled Indian paths. The proximity to the creek, and to the well-trod path, would allow customers to easily come by foot, horse or canoe. It would be the ideal place for Buchanan to turn his dreams into reality.

"Do you speak of that land around the bend?"

"That's the spot. I'd like to buy it, if I can."

"Ah, you have a good eye for land, Buchanan. Chief Tewea of the Lenape owns that. He is a good man. If you would like, I can introduce you to him and you can ask him about it."

"Is he friendly? Do you think he would sell his property to a white man?"

"If the price was generous, I believe he would sell anything he owned to anyone who asked," laughed the old man. "He's not foolish enough to turn down a profitable arrangement. It's too late in the evening to disturb him right now. Would you like to go and see him at dawn? He likes to start his day down by the big river and we could walk down there to see him before his day gets busy."

"Yes, I would."

Arthur was up before dawn, waiting and watching for Kish to emerge from his home. As soon as the chief was out in the open, Arthur walked over to greet him.

The men walked down to where the creek fed into the river. There, just as predicted, they found a dark, burly Lenape, magnificently dressed and gingerly wading in the creek, looking for fish. With his fishing spear in hand, he waited quietly for a large fish to swim within reach.

"Tewea," Kishacoquillas called out softly. "Friend, may we talk for a while?"

"Of course," came his even reply as he waded ashore. "Who is this with you?" Tewea eyed the newcomer up and down, assessing whether this exceptionally tall, muscular man before him might be a potential friend or a foe. He did not have the look of a pampered city dweller. Arthur's long gray hair was tied back like a warrior and his face was creased with age and exposure to the elements. This was a woodsman. He would have to talk to him for a while to determine whether he was a woodsman who could be trusted.

"Tewea, this is my old friend, Arthur Buchanan. Arthur, this is the great Lenape Chief, Tewea."

Arthur gently offered his hand, unsure whether the Indian would accept his gesture. Some locals would while others would not. Tewea recognized Arthur's name and knew his reputation to be a good one, so he accepted the extended hand without hesitation.

"It is a great honor to meet you, Chief Tewea."

"The honor is mine, Buchanan. I have heard your name before, and I have heard many good things about you."

"Buchanan has some matters that he would like to discuss with you. Would you come to my fire?" Tewea agreed and the three walked back to Kishacoquillas' hut.

Arthur broke out the flask of whiskey that he'd brought along for the occasion and passed it to his new acquaintance.

"What is it that you want from me, Buchanan," inquired a curious Tewea after downing his first healthy swig and passing the flask to Kish.

"Tewea, Kishacoquillas tells me that you own much of that land across the creek."

"I do. And?"

"I would like to buy a small piece of it from you if you are willing and if we can agree on a fair price."

"No. I do not want to sell it. Too many of your people want to buy land in this valley. If I don't put a stop to it, your people will soon outnumber my people." He was polite but steadfast in his decision.

"It is true that many of my people will want to come here. Your valley is one of the most beautiful I have ever seen. The land is fertile and the game plenty. Surely you can understand why the newcomers want to buy the land and live here in this paradise. Would you please reconsider? I will pay handsomely, more than any other man would." Arthur was mindful about what Kish had said, that Tewea might be open to a generous offer.

"No, I will not reconsider. I understand completely why white men want to buy our land, but I still have no interest in selling it to you. I want to keep the land for my people. No more white settlers."

"Chief Tewea, you are a great man. I respect your wisdom and your decision" Arthur handed him the flask again. Tewea nodded in acknowledgement of the whiskey and the flattering words.

While Arthur was wise enough to not argue, he wasn't about to give up his pursuit quite so easily. He understood before he even met this man that he might encounter some resistance. However, his charm and his patient persistence had won him many a lucrative deal in the past. He would not give up his efforts just yet. He must tread lightly, though, or he would risk making an enemy of Tewea and lose all hope of ever securing the land that he wanted. He remained calm and waited for an appropriate question to open the door to further conversation. It could not come from him. It would have to come from one of the two men before him. It didn't take long for it to come, though.

"Why here, Buchanan? The mountains are full of equally beautiful places to build a home. Why do you want my land in particular?"

"I want to build more than just a home for my family. I had hoped to buy some land here to build a trading post for the benefit of both our peoples. Honest, open trading brings good things to all people. When I ran a post over near Lancaster, your people and mine both profited. But I understand that this is not what you want in this valley, so I will not question your stand."

Arthur offered the flask once more as Tewea focused his deep-set, dark eyes on this strange white man. The chief was intrigued by the thought of not only making a profit on the sale of the land for himself but also the possibility of his people enjoying considerable profit in the trade business over the coming years. Profit for his people, and even more so himself, always intrigued him. Much like Buchanan, he was keenly aware of the endless possibilities that what Buchanan was suggesting might bring.

"Tell me how it is that you ran a business that profited both peoples."

"Well, here's how it worked over there: The Conestoga hunters would go out trapping and hunting, then bring me the pelts. They could exchange their pelts for other things they wanted, like cooking pots and guns and such. The white people work it the same way. They'd bring things that they had plenty of, or could make plenty of, and then they would trade for things that the tribes people would bring. Every man or woman could swap for the things that they wanted but couldn't otherwise get. Trade is good for all people. No one has to go without the things that they need or want as long as they engage in fair trade."

Tewea looked into the fire and tried to imagine the kind of business that Buchanan was describing. His people had long traded among each other and with other tribes but their interactions with the white people had been rather limited up to this point. The European settlers brought many new and useful items with them to the valley when they migrated from their cities in the east.

"And," continued Arthur, "Most of my customers lingered at the board a while to drink my whiskey, beer and hard cider. For a fair price, of course."

"Hmm," murmured an ever-so-slightly tipsy Tewea. He was mulling over the convenience of having certain goods readily accessible, especially European firearms. Being able to trade for food stuffs in the winter when the hunters might be struggling to provide for their families might well save many of them from starvation. What Buchanan was saying was starting to make sense.

Arthur sensed that the old chief's resolve was slowly melting. His special recipe Irish whiskey had a way of doing that to men. By now, the three men were relaxed and enjoying a friendly comradery around the fire. Arthur knew it was time to stop talking about his plans. He had smoothly transitioned from a failed plea to a heart-to-heart discussion of dreams. He could now see his own dreams being reflected in Tewea's eyes. If he didn't stop talking about it now and give him time to mull things over, the Chief might suspect him of restating his already rejected plea. If he didn't change the subject fast, he risked offending him.

"Chief Tewea, I have to tell you that you remind me a great deal of an old, burly Dutchman that used to spend many an evening at my table throwing back hard cider. Jacobs, his name was. Captain Jacobs. He was a very important man among our people. A man of great stature and great wisdom, much like yourself."

"Captain Jacobs," murmured Tewea, his eyes now heavy and his voice growing deeper and softer. His hard edges were now as soft as they had ever been.

"That's what I should call you - Captain Jacobs - because you are tall, strong and wise, just like him," exclaimed Buchanan. Chief Tewea, now also known as Captain Jacobs, tried but failed to conceal a thin smile. Buchanan had a way of watching people and quickly learning how to charm them into doing whatever it was that he wanted them to do. His honest but lavish praise, along with the sharing of Irish whiskey, was slowly winning over the reticent chief.

Kish had remained silent as he watched Arthur slowly win Tewea's confidence. He'd seen Buchanan work this special magic before. He was aware exactly what his old friend was doing but he wasn't concerned for his own people because Buchanan had a good heart to go with that sharp mind. Kish had never known him to raise a hand or a weapon against any man. Nor did he take anything that was not due him, as many white men would. Buchanan might be a shrewd negotiator but he was honest and trustworthy. Kish also wanted Arthur to build his trading post here near the village. It would be a good thing for the people of Ohesson.

"Tewea," murmured Kish.

"No, Kishacoquillas. I am Tewea no more. I am now Captain Jacobs," he laughed.

"Captain Jacobs, then," chortled Kishacoquillas. "Buchanan will not question your decision, but I will, my friend. I think you should reconsider. Think carefully about what he has said to you and what he is offering before you refuse him completely. You say you want no more white settlers, but what Buchanan would bring to this valley would be good for all who live here. Buchanan, I advise you to ask him once more." Arthur was greatly relieved that Kish had reopened the door for him.

"Alright, only because you insist, Kish, I will ask one more time. Captain Jacobs, would you sell me just a small piece of your land down by the creek? You can name your price."

"Alright Buchanan," he sighed. "You may buy some of my land. Tomorrow we will walk it together and talk. Your whiskey has dulled my mind. I can speak of it no more today."

Chapter Three

Arthur Buchanan was an extraordinarily intelligent and ambitious man, with an astute eye focused on the future. He was delighted that the land he'd been eyeing for nearly as long as he could remember was now legally his. This one, all important accomplishment, the securing of this land, laid the groundwork for making his most cherished dreams come true.

The first time Arthur saw Kishacoquillas Valley was on a crisp November day in 1735. Samuel Smith, the Sheriff of Lancaster, had recruited a large posse of young men to help him catch the infamous Thomas Cresap. Arthur Buchanan was among the recruits. Scouts reported that Cresap had recently built a cabin over near where the Juniata flowed into the Susquehanna. Samuel Smith wanted to arrest Cresap, even if it was the last thing that he ever did.

Cresap and his band of criminals had been wreaking havoc all around the countryside for several years. He raided the homes of Indians and whites alike, taking whatever he wanted whenever he wanted it, and eventually destroying whatever remained that he didn't want or couldn't carry. The sheriff and his two-dozen recruits rode off, determined to stop this brazen criminal before he could widen his wake of destruction.

Smith found Cresap's cabin exactly where it was reported to be. They approached slowly and peacefully, staying on their mounts. The ever-watchful Cresap had seen them approaching for quite a while and he was standing on the porch as they neared his cabin.

"What can I help you gentlemen with today," asked an overly friendly Cresap, trying to look calm and at ease. There was no hiding his edginess, though. It was obvious that they were there to take him in but he was playing them for time while he formulated an escape plan. He always had multiple escape plans in mind but he needed a minute or two to decide which one would provide the greatest chance for success in this particular situation.

"Thomas Cresap, we're here to bring you in for criminal behavior and take you before a judge in Philadelphia," announced Sheriff Smith. "Why don't you just get on your horse and come along peaceable with us. It'll go a lot easier for you if you do cooperate."

"Well now," answer Cresap. "I'm not sure I'm of a mind to do that. I ain't done nothing wrong for you to haul me in for."

"Cresap, everybody knows you've been running around thieving and killing and destroying folks' property. We aim to put a stop to that right here and right now."

"Now Sheriff, I ain't done anything that you all ain't been doing yourselves. Sure, I've killed me some Indians but only if they come after me first. And if they happened to have some valuable or interesting items in their possession, I'll bring 'em home after the fight. Ain't that what everybody's been doing around here these past few years? Why is it you're calling me a criminal when I'm no different from anybody else?"

Cresap surveyed the crowd before him, looking for a familiar face to appeal to. It didn't take long for him to recognize Arthur and he turned on the charm the minute he saw him.

"Hey, ho! If it isn't young Buchanan," he cried out, flashing a brown-stained smile. "I know you! We used to trade over in Lancaster. And I used to go sit at your brother Roberts's table and have a drink with him every once in a while. Been a long time since I saw you, young man. Why don't you come in and sit at my table a spell? It'd give me pleasure to serve you in my home. All of ya. Come on in and have a drink with me. I've plenty to go around."

Arthur shook his head in disgust and waited for the sheriff to answer.

"Cresap, we're not here on a social visit. Now go get your hat, mount up and come with us or we'll make you come with us."

"Sheriff, I'm just not inclined to do that today."

"I don't care what you're inclined to do. You're coming with us and that's all there is to it. You can either come voluntarily or we'll take you by force."

"Alright Sheriff," he sighed, seemingly resolved to his fate. "Whatever you say. Let me go in and grab my hat and tell the missus where I'm heading off to." He turned and walked into his cabin, bolting the door behind him.

"He ain't coming back out," said John Kelly.

"I didn't really expect him to. We got no choice now," remarked Sheriff Smith. "Let's burn him out boys. Set a fire over there by the window. We want him to come out alive so don't start it in front of the door." What Sheriff Smith didn't count on was that Cresap's cabin had a back door that was well hidden by a row of trees. Mrs. Cresap had run out the back and up the hill while Mr. Cresap was talking to the Smith and his posse, stalling them so that she could get a head start. As soon as Sheriff Smith had made it plain that they would not succumb to his charms, Mr. Cresap had turned and followed her immediately after he'd latched the front cabin door. He was nearly over the hill before Smith's men could light the fire.

"Too late for that Sheriff. He's already out the back and running. He's already up there on that ridge," reported David Priestly, directing everyone's attention to Cresap's backside just as he disappeared over the top of the hill.

"Let's go get him boys," ordered the Sheriff and the men rode off after him. Cresap and his wife were both on foot and couldn't outrun the horses. They put up a good fight but both were subdued in a matter of minutes.

"We've got to get them over to Philadelphia and that's a long ride back. Let's see what there is to eat in the cabin and maybe have us some grub before we go. He said he had plenty of drink to go around. Let's see if that's true and if there's plenty of food to go with it."

"What of Mrs. Cresap," asked Arthur. "He is charged with many a crime but I don't know that she is. Do we take her in or leave her here?"

"I think it's best we take her along. She might not be charged with any crimes, but we don't know what she'd be likely to do if we let her go. She might round up some of his old cronies and ambush us along the road. She looks to be a pretty tough cookie, herself. Let's keep them both tied up till we get them back to Philadelphia. I wouldn't trust either one of them as far as I could throw them."

The posse raided the raider's cabin and found a generous store of both food and whiskey. While men sat eating, drinking and congratulating themselves for catching Cresap, Arthur decided to take a long walk and explore the stunning countryside. He climbed up Cresap's escape ridge and took a look at beauty that spread out before him for miles and miles. The blue-green hills reminded him of Ireland and he was immediately smitten.

This lush valley looked like *The Promised Land* to Arthur. Two big rivers ran through the basin and Arthur was certain that they were brimming with fish. There were plenty of trees to provide lumber for building and the soil looked to be rich enough to grow any crop a fellow had a mind to grow. There was plenty of game to hunt so there would be plenty of food to eat and furs to trade. The posse had travelled here on well-worn Indian trails that would one day make travelling relatively easy for pioneers heading west. While the other men in the posse were drinking and thinking about getting back home,

Arthur was dreaming about one day making this wonderful valley his home.

As soon as the Cresaps had been delivered to Philadelphia and their mission complete, Sheriff Smith disbanded the posse and sent the men back to their normal lives. Instead of going back to his life in Lancaster, Arthur opted to return to the land of his dreams. He wanted to spend some time there and find out for himself whether it actually was all that he believed it to be. He needed to walk the land and get a true feel for it. He had to be sure that his first impression of the place was accurate. He planned to spend a good amount of time hunting and trapping while exploring the area. Once he had a goodly cache, he'd go back to Philadelphia and sell it all. He hoped to turn a large enough profit from trapping to build a wonderous life in that magical place.

Chapter Four

Arthur was in no way disappointed with what he found during his expeditions. He didn't go back just once. In fact, he made so many trips in and out of Kish Valley that he'd lost count. Every time he went into the valley, he'd explore a new area. Each time he came out, he'd be weighed down with a load of furs so massive that his horse could barely carry it. He memorized every detail of both banks of the Juniata, as well as every tributary that fed it. He explored each cave that he stumbled upon, oftentimes sleeping in one for protection from the elements. He made friends with the local tribes and would bring them goods from the east that they asked for. Arthur believed deep down in his soul that this was where God meant for him to be.

In later years, Arthur would look back and wonder if he'd have ever found this place had he not come on that sheriff's mission. He firmly believed that life was a series of stepping stones; that each step in life led him to where he was meant to be in the end. Had he not gone to Lancaster to sell a load of furs, he would have missed being recruited by Sheriff Smith. Had the posse not returned to Lancaster, landing him inside the tavern that afternoon, he might never have met Dorcas. He was always grateful for that stepping stone, that single posse ride, that had opened up a whole new world of dreams and possibilities for the future.

Before he met Dorcas, Arthur assumed he would carve out his life in the wilderness as a bachelor. His vision increased in scope when he married Dorcas and it increased even more with each child they brought into the world. Now he was eager to make every last plan a reality with the help of his beloved Dorcas and the family that they had created. He believed that they could do just about anything they wanted to do as long as they all worked together.

Arthur wasn't interested in anything the least bit humble. His big vision demanded that he build a big house. He was building a dynasty that would endure and no rough-hewn, one-room cabin would do. This was to be more than a mere trading post. His intention was to create an establishment that would be the center of commerce for the whole valley.

Arthur's intention was to be the lord of it all, just as his Buchanan ancestors had been over their lands back in Scotland. Many generations of Buchanan men had severed as Lairds of

Drummikill and Arthur was proud of his lineage. His forefathers were visionaries, warriors and leaders. He meant to continue that proud legacy and to pass it on to his own sons. He would see to it that all the boys, including his Holt stepsons, would exemplify the Buchanan clan motto, *Brighter, hence the honour.* It was Arthur's belief that all men ought to strive to that high ideal.

Most early American settlers built simple one or two-room cabins. The largest might have a loft if there were children. When the Buchanans lived over in Lancaster, their home was small because his parcel of land was small. Here by the creek, he could spread out as far as he wanted. When Arthur and the boys built the main house, they built an imposing, two-story log structure designed to be a trading post on the first floor and a home to the Buchanan family on the second. Never before had any white settler built anything of this scope so far out in the wilds.

Arthur had always been a tad envious of the grand houses he'd seen in Philadelphia and that was the model that he built his house upon. Wide stone fireplaces commanded each end of the building on both floors, providing ample heat and light throughout the building. In the front room that would serve as the tavern and trading post, multiple candle sconces lined the long walls. Three hanging chandeliers ran the length of the room. When the fireplaces, the candles in the chandelier and the wall sconces were all lit, a bright, warm glow was reflected on the polished wood floors below and shone deep into the corners of the room. The Buchanan place was as bright as midday no matter what the time of day or the weather. Even when none of the fires were lit, glass pane windows, brought all the way from Philadelphia, graced the front of the tavern, allowing remarkable amounts of afternoon sun to warm and brighten the room.

Arthur spent a great deal of his savings furnishing the place, ordering a large shipment of tables and chairs from the city. A long, wooden table anchored the center of the gathering space and several small, round tables were scattered about. At the furthest corner from the entry, next to the door leading to the kitchen, stood the wooden stall from which Arthur Buchanan would conduct business, hold court and survey his new empire.

A roomy kitchen sat behind the serving room and Dorcas was pleased with the room that she would have to work in. She was going to need every bit of that space as soon as the customers started filling that front room. Arthur built floor to ceiling shelves for the pots, pans and serving dishes that were being shipped from Boston. Dorcas herself had insisted on a ten-foot long work table.

On the day they were set to officially open for business, the happy couple stepped out into the morning mist to admire their new establishment. Every surface, inside and out, had been painted or polished to a high gleam.

"Something's missing," declared Dorcas, cocking her head and surveying the area, trying to figure out what was off. The white house with black shutters looked wonderful to her but it needed something more, but she couldn't quite put her finger on what that might be.

"I haven't put up the sign yet. That's what's missing," declared Arthur.

"Ah, that's it. Just looks like a big house without a sign. Did you have a name in mind?"

"Well, I was thinking maybe *Buchanans'*."

"But your brother William has always used the family name on his place. Don't you want something different? Something unique to you?"

"Well, it is the family name, and I am proud of it. You don't like our family name?"

"Don't be silly. I'm just as proud of the name as you are but I think we ought to name it something different. The place you ran in Carlisle with your brother had the family name and that was fine, but this is our place and I think it high time we picked a new name. It's going to be different from what folks are used to seeing and the name should be different, too. I intend to spend the rest of my natural days here and I'd like to give it a special name. A special name for a special place."

"A special name, huh? I'm not sure that the name matters all that much but what do you have in mind?"

"Let me think on it a minute."

"Back home in Monaghan, there were a lot of places with names like *The Red Lion* and *The Copper Kettle*," he suggested.

"Those are far too common," she answered. "We want to be different."

"To set us apart from all the other taverns in the valley? Dorcas, we're the only business for miles around. We don't need to be different."

"But I *want* us to be different. Hush a minute and let me think," she snapped. Dorcas eyed the massive house, considering the matter for several minutes before she spoke again. Arthur knew to pick his battles with Dorcas carefully and he could clearly see that this one wasn't going to be worth fighting. A slight smile warming her face and a twinkle dancing in her eye told Arthur that she had a most worthy idea.

"You remember that big, old, black elk that used to swim down in the river?"

"Yup. The biggest elk I ever saw in my life."

"How about *The Bounding Elk*?"

"*The Bounding Elk.* Hmmm." Arthur stroked his thick white beard. "*The Bounding Elk.* Sounds . . . powerful. And I never heard tell of another place with that name. I do like that name. *The Bounding Elk.* Just to be different. And to make you happy."

"Alright then. You cut a big piece of wood for me, and I'll paint us up a real nice sign. Make sure it is big enough to hold the whole name."

"What are you going to paint it with?"

"I've got some red paint that someone brought in a while back. That ought to do well enough."

That afternoon, Arthur hung the freshly painted sign above the door and with that, *The Bounding Elk* was officially open for business. The tavern was ready to leave its mark on history, whatever that mark might be. They'd been conducting their trading business out in the yard as the house was being built, but now they could do really do it up right. Now they could serve food and drink and make it a real proper tavern.

The Buchanans didn't have to wait long for their first customers. Their trading friends had been anxiously awaiting this day. Arthur and Dorcas welcomed all who came to their door. Ohesson's native residents came to trade, as did the fur trappers from the countryside and the settlers who had recently moved into the valley. Arthur rapidly developed a reputation for fair dealing and uncommon hospitality that both the natives and the newcomers deeply appreciated.

Many customers crossed the Buchanan threshold looking for far more than fur trading services. They would come from miles around to do business with Buchanan but they would stay long after their business was concluded to socialize with their neighbors, exchange bits of news and to enjoy Dorcas's considerable cooking skills. Folks felt at home there. They felt welcome and they felt safe. *The Bounding Elk* made one and all feel like a part of a larger community, no matter how far they had to travel to walk through that door.

From the break of dawn until several hours past dusk, there was rarely a quiet moment within those walls. All sorts of folks gathered around those tables. The faces found within were both young and old, both pale and tan. Some visitors dressed in buckskin and some were garbed in fine woven woolens. Appearance didn't matter at *The Bounding Elk*. Everyone was treated with the same welcome and the same respect regardless of what they wore.

Hungry, lonely men who came to the area ahead of their families regularly gathered around the long plank table, eating and talking. Men of all backgrounds leaned on the trading counter throwing back pints and conducting business, while Arthur kept a watchful eye on his kingdom from behind the bar. Dorcas was like a charming, whirling dervish, running madly between the kitchen and the tables, making sure that each visitor always had a full plate and an equally full tankard.

Anything worth hearing would be heard at the Buchanan place. Travelers passing through brought news with them from Boston and from Philadelphia. The trappers and Shawnee brought news from the western wilds. The news they brought was important. More than once, it was lifesaving.

The French, the English, the German and the Scotch-Irish were all trying to carve out new lives in this new world and they were all willing to fight for the way of life that they had a mind to create. Knowing where the enemy troops and aggressive tribes were advancing, not to mention when they might be expected to be in the vicinity, was crucial to everyone's survival. Life along the creek appeared to be peaceful and secure, but trouble always lurked somewhere not too far away.

Chapter Five
1756

In middle of an usually snowy February, the Buchanans closed the tavern, packed up the whole family and made a rare trip to Lancaster for the wedding of their son, Thomas. He was betrothed to Miss Elizabeth Mitchell, the youngest daughter of John and Jane Mitchell, close friends of the Buchanans. John and Arthur had known each other for many years, and Jane met Dorcas on the day that the Buchanans wed. They'd been neighbors for many years and it predictably followed that their children would become fast and lasting friends. It seemed only natural that Thomas and Elizabeth would marry, since they had known and cared for each other nearly all their lives. All four parents were understandably pleased with the match.

Dorcas wasn't quite so pleased with having to travel in the freezing February air but the winter months were when most weddings traditionally took place. Wintertime was a sensible time for weddings and such because the men weren't needed in the fields at that time of the year.

"Sure you don't mind making this trip, Dorkey," asked Arthur.

"You know that I don't. Much as I hate this cold, I'd hate it much more if I had to miss this wedding." She would have traveled anywhere, anytime for her children. A team of wild horses couldn't keep Dorcas from anything having to do with any one of them. "I just hope the rest of them get married closer to home, like Henry did," she commented as she wrapped a blanket tighter around her shoulders. Henry had married his lovely Sarah before one of the fireplaces in the tavern because her folks were neighbors to the Buchanans.

"The only way that you can make sure that happens is to marry them off to neighbor families and we don't have too awfully many neighbors to choose from these days."

"I wish we could arrange that, but you know how young love is. I swear I knew when Thomas and Elizabeth were just knee-high to a grasshopper that they would eventually marry. I just knew it. They were partial to each other from the very beginning. Neither one of them has ever had eyes for anyone else at all."

"They have always been particularly partial to one another, haven't they?"

"Hmm. No question about that," she agreed. "It does make sense that they want to be married at Lancaster. Most brides want to be married at their own parents' places. Most bride's mothers dream and plan for the big day years before it actually comes." She didn't want to admit to Arthur that she already harbored dreams for their own daughter's big day, even though it was likely a good eight to ten years away. "I don't mind traveling all that much, really. I don't like being away from home and I don't care for this cold but travelling isn't all that bad."

"Not all that bad, huh? I think you loathe travelling but it's not in your nature to complain, so you won't admit it."

"There's no use in complaining about anything. Complaining doesn't make things one bit better. Besides, we are much better suited to travel out through this wilderness than John and Jane Mitchel would be. They haven't ventured out of Lancaster since I can't remember when. I'd worry about their safety if they tried to travel to our place. We've done it plenty of times and know what kind of trouble to look out for where they wouldn't."

"You make a good point there. We are much better hands at it and better able to travel these roads than they are. God knows we've traveled them enough times to know each and every curve and bump in the road. We also know where to look for trouble, be it highwaymen or critters, and how to handle it if we come across it. I just can't imagine Jane Mitchell toughing out this trip. She might be alright, but I still can't imagine it."

"Mm," she murmured in agreement. "It just doesn't seem possible that Thomas is getting married already. Seems like just yesterday he was a mere freckle-faced little boy, spending his days getting into orneriness down on the creek."

"He's 22 years old now. It's been a while since he got into any orneriness. Any that we know of, anyway," chuckled Arthur.

"I'm afraid it won't be too many more years before these three will be getting hitched," she said, tilting her head toward Arthur, Jr., William, Jane and Robert who were dozing off under piles of quilts in the back of the wagon.

"That time will be here before we know it," he agreed.

Chapter Six

Jane Mitchell came rushing out the front door to meet their guests the minute the wagon appeared in front of the familiar brick home on Queen Street. She was so anxious to meet her guests that she ran out into the cold without a coat.

"Oh, we're so happy to see you," exclaimed Jane, still wiping her hands and straightening her dress as she ran out to embrace Dorcas. "You must be freezing from that long ride. You all come in now and warm yourselves in front of the fire. I've laid out some food for everyone, too. You must be absolutely famished."

"I am," hollered William.

"Me, too," cried Robert.

"Now you boys mind your manners," chided Dorcas.

"Oh, don't go worrying about that, Dorcas. Your children are always well-behaved. You've raised them right."

"Hmm. I hope so but time will tell won't it," she countered. "You children get the bags and bring them into the house and up the stairs."

"Yes, Momma," they replied in unison.

"Where's Armstrong," asked Jane.

"He'll be riding in tomorrow. Now Jane, tell me what can I do to help?"

"First, I want you to get warm and eat. We have everything under control here. There's lots of little things left to be done later, but first let's chat and catch-up. We have plenty of hands here to get things done for tomorrow. I haven't seen you in for far too long and I can't tell you how much that I've longed for your company."

John Mitchell came up around the side yard and extended his hand in greeting to his oldest friend.

"Arthur, old man! So glad to see you." The handshake instantly morphed into a bear hug.

"It's so good to see you, John."

"Let's take your rig round back and get your horses seen to, then we'll join the women folk. Of course, we'll stop off on the back porch and have us a wee dram before we go in," he said, winking at his friend.

"Jane, where are the bride and groom," asked Dorcas as they walked into the long hall and hung up their coats.

"Elizabeth went down to May's to get something for her hair. She's getting the jitters and now she's suddenly decided that the combs she picked out weeks ago are all wrong." The women chuckled knowingly. "Honestly, I think she just wanted to get out of the house and walk off some of her nerves."

"And my son, the groom?"

"Like most men before the wedding, he's down at the pub with his friends. They did their long ride in two days ago, meeting and drinking with all their friends along the way. I hope that he's sober enough to stand before the preacher come tomorrow," Jane joked.

"Well, if he's not, we'll just have to hold him up long enough to get through the vows," laughed Dorcas. "Do you think there's any way that we can send our husbands down there later to join the younger men and get them out of our way so that we can get things done?"

"I already told John that he should go show Arthur the new pub down the street."

"Ah, Jane. You are a wise woman in indeed. You're always thinking two steps ahead of the need. Now, what's left to be done?"

"I think that I have everything well under control, but your help and your company will be a blessing, nonetheless. You'll be a great help just keeping me to calm my own nerves. Let's go back in the kitchen and get on it, but let's keep our spirits high and start off with a wee dram to get things going, just you and me."

"Ah you read my mind," answered Dorcas.

"Great minds think alike, my dear friend."

Both families were in high spirits long before they indulged in their drams. Like the Buchanans, the Mitchells were thrilled beyond measure with the match. What could be better than having their daughter wed to the son of their dearest friends? And to share grandchildren? What a blessing it would be for everyone.

John and Jane had been preparing for the wedding for several days and now the Buchanan family rolled up their sleeves and got to work helping with the final preparations. The walls of the Mitchell house positively vibrated with love and joyous comradery.

Jane and Dorcas baked cakes and breads, and roasted turkey, ham and venison. The older children pushed the furniture back in the dining and sitting rooms, then set up makeshift tables that the Mitchell men had built earlier in the week. All the men worked together to prepare the gallons of ale, whiskey and madeira that the wedding guests were expected to consume during the coming days.

After a hasty breakfast on the morning of the wedding, while the women were primping and fussing over the bride, Dorcas instructed the men to go check on the state of the Saint James Episcopal Church around the corner on Duke Street, where the ceremony was to be had. The men were relieved to have a valid excuse to get away from the house for a while. Fussing women tended to make both Arthur and John quite uncomfortable.

"Arthur, you go check on the church. Make sure that floor is swept and there's a good fire in the fireplace. We can't have folks getting cold during the wedding."

"I'll be glad to do that. It'll do us good to get away from all the female foolishness going on upstairs."

"And we'll be just as thankful to have you out from underfoot. Take William and Robert with you, too. Get them out of the house. We don't need any of your sort around just now."

"Our sort? And just what might you mean by that, woman?"

"Menfolk. We don't need any menfolk under foot."

"Speaking of menfolk, I just realized that I didn't see the man of the hour, Thomas, at breakfast this morning. He didn't turn tail and run, did he" joked John.

"I believe he had better raising than that," countered the groom's mother.

"All I know is that Dorcas would tan his hide if he did do something like that," Arthur chimed in.

"Oh, he never would do that. I have it on good authority that he and his friends tucked in last night over at Jacob Stackpole's place. They thought it would be better to stay over there rather than risk waking the rest of us when they came stumbling in during the wee hours. The truth more likely is that he didn't want to risk us all seeing him in such a state," explained John.

"Smart boy, that one." John and Arthur smiled at each other knowingly. They both had enjoyed their own raucous adventures during their younger years, particularly in the days leading up to each of their weddings.

"Looks like we needn't have bothered coming to check," remarked Arthur. The men walked into the church to find the floors freshly swept and a healthy fire already heating the main floor. All that the men had to do was to fill the wall sconces with the new candles that Jane had sent along with them. She wanted everything perfect for her daughter's wedding and she would not have half-burnt candles dulling the sanctuary where her daughter was to be married.

"I knew that all along. Reverend Locke is as good man as ever walked God's green earth. I knew he'd have everything in right order. The women just wanted us out of the house. Truth be known, I was glad of any excuse to get out of there and away from the hubbub. But what say? Shall we go back to the house now so that we can escort the ladies back for the ceremony?"

"Aye, but let's not rush it. It's a short walk and we have plenty of time. I don't want to get into the middle of any more of that female fussing about. I have no patience for that."

"Agreed."

The men took their time and enjoyed a leisurely stroll back to the house. They stepped into the house's warm entryway just as the Elizabeth, Jane and Dorcas were descending the stairs. The two gentlemen helped the women into their wraps and took them by the arm for the short walk to the church, followed by their younger children.

When they arrived, Thomas and his friends were waiting for them on the steps in front of the church. Reverend Locke greeted them and led the procession into the small sanctuary. Thomas and Elizabeth followed the minister, with their closest friends in tow as attendants. The Mitchells and Buchanans filed in behind them, trailed by their extended family and other wedding guests.

"Friends, let us begin," declared the robed minister as everyone took their places. He opened his book and read, "Dearly beloved, we are gathered together here in the sight of God, and in the face of this congregation, to join together this man and this woman in holy matrimony . . ."

Arthur, Jr., William and Robert fidgeted, anxious to leave the ceremony and get to the feast and the fun that awaited them. Jane sat snuggled up next to her mother, dreaming of the day when she would take her turn as a bride before the altar. As Thomas slipped a ring onto Elizabeth's left hand, Dorcas dabbed at her eyes, using her late mother's handkerchief and wishing that her mother, daughter Jane's name keep, could be there to see this wonderful day. Arthur squeezed her free hand and gave her a warm, loving smile. Dorcas often hid her softer side during their day-to-day challenges but even she could not keep up a tough façade during these moments. Arthur smiled gently at her. He found her womanly tears to be completely endearing, especially since they were so rarely witnessed.

When the ceremony was over, the entire assembly walked the short distance back to the Mitchell home for the reception. Long known as generous and jovial hosts, John and Jane Mitchell had spared no expense for their daughter's wedding. They beckoned their guests to the drawing room and adjoining dining room, where tables and sideboards lining the walls of both rooms groaned under the weight of food and drink.

Members of both families doted on the bride, the groom, the guests and each other alike as the afternoon melted into evening. The father of the bride and the father of the groom, along with the uncles and grown brothers on both sides, took turns giving toasts and speeches. Children played games in the hallway and spilled out into the front yard in unrestrained merriment. Couples danced in the drawing room. Old men told riveting stories in front of the fire, while old women snuck off to the kitchen and back hall to gossip. The festivities carried on throughout the afternoon and well into the night, until everyone retired to their beds and collapsed from joyous exhaustion.

The entire Buchanan family stayed with the Mitchells for two days after the wedding, long after the other guests had departed. Just a few months prior to the wedding, Armstrong, Arthur, Jr., Thomas and Henry helped their father build the newlyweds a sturdy log cabin near the tavern in Kish Valley. Arthur and Dorcas wanted to make sure that the bride and groom were escorted to their new home.

"Momma," chided Elizabeth, "There is absolutely no more room in the wagon. We can't squeeze in even one more tiny thing."

"But your grandmother's quilt. Don't you want to take it? If there's no room, just put it across your lap to keep you warm while you ride." Jane was pleased that her daughter was now married to a good and honest man, but at the same time, she was despondent that her girl was moving so far away. She couldn't resist lathering on some motherly attention for few more moments.

"Oh, alright, I'll take it." Elizabeth was right about the lack of room for any additions to the wagon. It was packed to the brim with her hope chest, their wedding gifts and everything else her parents thought she might need or want in her new home.

"Jane, don't you go worrying about your girl," said Dorcas. "We'll keep a good eye on her. Their place is well within sight of ours. We'll be right there any time that she wants us – and probably many times when she doesn't."

"I know that, Dorcas. I appreciate it. I really do."

"And if you have a mind to, you can come visit in the spring. We'll be glad to put you up for a while so you can see for yourself just how well they're getting on." Jane smiled through her tears at her old friend.

"I'll do just that, Dorcas. You just count on seeing me at your door in a few weeks." Dorcas thought about her earlier conversation with Arthur and wondered if the Mitchells would ever make that rough journey. It was hard to tell. Dorcas would do anything for her children, and she could truly envision Jane braving the wilderness for Elizabeth.

Chapter Seven

A few weeks after the wedding, as the newlyweds were settling into life by the creek and spring was starting to make an appearance, an old fur trapping friend of Arthur's appeared at the tavern.

"Michael Brown," called out Arthur. "What brings you here, friend? You out trapping?"

"I was but now I'm turning tail and heading back towards Lancaster. I heard there were troubles around these parts, and I intend to stay as far away from any troubles as I can."

"What troubles?"

"Word has it that the Sioux and Ottawa tribes are on the war path. They're convinced that the English settlers are going to take all of their land and word has it they're attacking every cabin and settlement in their path."

"Do you know what direction they're heading?"

"I don't know for sure. That's why I'm heading to Lancaster. I figure I'm better off in any town of that size than I would be out in any woods by myself. I just hope that I can make it there without crossing their paths."

"Well, Michael, neither you nor I particularly like being in the city but that's probably the best place to be if you want to keep your scalp attached to your head. At least for now."

"What about you, Buchanan? You going to run or are you going to stay put for a while?"

"I'm not going to run just yet. We've got our own little town going here, so it's not like we're out here all alone. There is some security to be found in numbers, even in our small number. Still, I keep a sharp eye out for trouble every day. I've got many friends among the tribes here and they'll let me know if trouble's heading this way."

Buchanan's friendship with all sides did indeed provide him with great advantage, particularly his friendship with his friends from the local tribes. Shawnee and Lenape alike trusted and cared about him and they kept him apprised of any impending danger from unfriendly tribes and warring invaders.

A few weeks after the Michael Brown's visit, Chief Logan walked through the door of Buchanan's tavern seeking out his treasured friend.

"Logan! I haven't seen you in a long, long time," said Arthur. He noticed that a troubled look darkened the chief's face and that he wasn't quite as cheerful as he normally was when he rolled into the tavern.

"I've been out on the trail for a while. Buchanan, I am afraid that I have unfortunate news for you."

"What worries you, Logan?"

"Bad trouble is coming this way. You must take your family and run. The French and the Lenape are working together and attacking white settlers all over the valley."

"Do you know where they are now?"

"They are well north and west of Fort Granville by about 40 miles, so you probably have enough time to escape. Go now, though. If I were you, I'd go back to Carlisle. The trails over that way are clear. Go now – right this minute. If you hesitate, you and your kin could be in considerable danger."

"Even me? Why, I've always be a friend to all people, no matter what their tribe."

"Most of these warriors are coming from parts far away from here and they don't know you like the locals do. And, I am sad to say that in times of trouble, even old friends can become new enemies. It saddens me greatly to tell you that the man you call Captain Jacobs is leading some tribes in these raids. He takes direction from the French officers but he is leading his own people in these violent attacks."

"Jacobs? Why, I bought this land from him. He's sat right here at this table many, many times."

"I know that but now he has turned. The French have convinced him that the English mean to destroy all the tribes and take the land for themselves."

"But I bought my land from him fair and square. All the folks I know bought their land fair and square. They didn't steal it. And neither me nor my family have ever raised a hand against him nor any of his people."

"I know that, and you know that, but the fact is that he is fuming mad that so many white men are coming to the valley, and he blames you, in part, for bringing them here. There really is no time to discuss this further. Gather your family and go right now. Tell every white settler you know that, if they value their lives, they must leave the valley immediately."

"Logan, thank you for warning me, Logan. I will go but I hope that we can return in peace someday."

"That is my hope, as well. I will try to protect your home here. I'll tell them that it belongs to me now because I took it from you. I'll stay here for a few days to make it look as though I am actually living here. That might at least stop them from burning it to the ground." The two shook hands and the chief took his leave. As Arthur watched him go, he wondered if they would ever again ever meet face-to-face.

Horace and four other men had been playing cards and talking when the chief came in. They watched intently, attempting to listen to the conversation as Logan and Arthur had put their heads together.

They waited patiently for Arthur to share his news. As soon as his old friend left, Arthur walked as stoically as he could to the table and relayed what he had just been told.

"Men, we need to move out of here. The trail south is clear for now, but it won't be for long. Go home and get your families and head out fast as you can." His voice was steady but firm. "Horace, you come and ride along with me and my family. I don't want you on that trail alone. You can ride in one of the wagons if you want to, but you might want to go back and get your old mare to carry you and a pack of your belongings. You can't count on coming back to anything you leave behind. You go and get what you need but hurry right back. We'll wait on you."

"It won't take me long to pack because I don't own much of any value. I'll get my things and be back before you have time to hitch up your wagons."

The alarmed men rushed toward the door and their respective homes to save what little they could in the few moments allotted to their safe removal.

Chapter Eight

Arthur found Dorcas out behind the tavern, walking back from the smokehouse with a large ham cradled in her arms.

"Dorcas, we have to run back to Carlisle for a while and we have to go quick as we can go." Her eyes went wide with surprise and the color drained from her cheeks.

"What? What happened, Arthur?"

"Chief Logan just told me that Captain Jacobs and his people are unhappy with the new settlers and they're attacking white folks' cabins and settlements all across the valley. They're showing no mercy to any white man, woman or child, so we can't risk staying here. Let's load up and get going."

"Now? The whole household?"

"No, there's no time for that. Just pack up that ham and any food that you can and fill some water jugs. Grab some clothes and whatever else you can get lightening quick. We're not risking our lives by loading up furniture and dishes. We need to get going. There's no telling when the raiders will get to this area. I'll run over and tell Henry and Thomas and get them going, too. We should all to ride together in case we come across trouble on the trail to Carlisle. They say the path is clear for now, but things could change fearfully fast."

"Surely your old friends wouldn't hurt us? Surely not when all we've ever done has been to be good to them."

"I'd like to think that they wouldn't harm us but, at times like this you never know. Logan said Jacobs is right at the heart of it. Enough talk. We can discuss it later. Let's get moving."

"Jacobs? Oh my, no. I can't even imagine it. How could he," she questioned before her resolve kicked in. "Alright, then. I'll gather up the children and whatever we can carry and throw it all into the wagon. I'll hook up the team while you're getting the boys. We'll all be ready right quick." He gave her a terse nod and headed out the door to his stepsons' homes to share the news and spur them to action. Behind him, he heard Dorcas resolutely calling their younger children to grab things and get to the wagon. He knew that, even though she was carrying on and doing exactly what she needed to do, her heart was breaking at the thought of their old friend's surprising betrayal.

Henry and Thomas had been working the field out behind their adjoining cabins since daybreak and were taking a break under a shade tree when

Arthur came riding up. Both young men looked at their stepfather with deep concern in their eyes. Arthur usually walked the mile to their places, but it was obvious that this visit was one of urgency. Arthur didn't even bother to dismount his ride.

"Boys, hostile tribes are coming, and we got to get out of here as fast as we can. We are in true danger. Get your guns. Load up your families, some food and water and some clothes. No time for furniture, dishes or other nonsense. Take nothing but what you absolutely have to have. Get your wagons loaded up and back over to my place fast as you can."

"How long do you think we'll be staying there," asked Tom.

"I don't know. We'll work that out later. Let's move while we are still able," he called out with an increasingly frantic edge to his voice. The harsh reality of the situation was starting to sink in, and he was becoming edgy with fear for his family. He turned his horse and galloped back to his own home. Tom and Henry jumped up and grabbed the guns that had been leaning against the tree beside them.

"Tom, I'll get my wagon and come around to fetch you and Elizabeth. We'll move faster if we don't take too many wagons, so you just leave yours for now. Should we be ambushed, we'll be able to protect the women and children better if they are in one wagon."

"We'll be ready when you are."

Henry burst into the door of his small cabin.

"Sarah, gather up the baby and his things. Wrap up the clothes in the quilt and throw it in the back of the wagon when I bring it round front. We have to run because Indians are coming."

"Lord have mercy, no!" she cried in horror.

"Do it now. Quick as you can. Hurry, hurry," he exclaimed as he grabbed a basket and filled it with the water jugs and some grub left from breakfast. He ran out and threw the basket in the back of the wagon and his shotgun up in the seat. He hurriedly hooked up his team and pulled the wagon to the front of the house just as Sarah, pale with fear, came out with a quilt full of what few supplies she could grab. Tears were streaming down her face, and she looked ready to faint from fear.

"It'll be alright, Sarah. Let's just keep moving. You come get the baby and I'll get the cradle, so that he can ride warm and dry out of the weather behind the wagon seat. Let's go. Pa's waiting for us at his place."

His wife ran back into the house and grabbed her sleeping child, holding him as close as humanly possible to her breast. She climbed in behind the seat of the wagon where Henry had nestled the cradle and gently tucked in the slumbering baby. She settled in next to her precious bundle and hovered protectively over the cradle, whispering a prayer a heartfelt prayer.

"Tom, you all ready yet," Henry called toward his brother's cabin.

"You know that I am, brother."

Thomas and Elizabeth threw some bundles of clothes wrapped in quilts, along with what little food they were able to grab into the back of the wagon and Elizabeth climbed in next to Sarah. Thomas climbed into the jump into the seat next to his brother, his long rifle riding ready across his lap.

"Let's go," Henry declared as he urged his horses on.

By the time they reached the main house, Dorcas and Arthur had loaded up their wagon with the children and a few meager supplies, and they were now arguing over whether or not to take the cow.

"We'll need her when we get to Carlisle, Arthur. We're leaving a lot behind; I'll not leave my cow."

"She'll slow us down, Dorcas."

"No, she won't. She's still pretty young and she has enough get up and go to keep up with the wagons. She wouldn't be able to keep up with horseback riders but she'll be able to keep up with the wagons."

There was no arguing with this woman once she set her mind to something. It was obvious that her mind was set on this matter, regardless of how foolish it might be to his mind.

"Have it your way. But, we'll hook her up behind the last wagon. If she can't keep up, we'll cut her loose and leave her on the path."

"She'll keep up. Don't you worry about it. I know my girl," she said as she defiantly hooked Bess to the back of the wagon. "Don't you worry, dear. We're not going to leave you out here all alone," she whispered to the bovine, affectionately stroking its nose.

Arthur, astride his horse, surveyed the scene to make sure that everything was arranged as it should be. Fourteen-year-old William sat in the driver's seat of his father's wagon, reins in hand, waiting for his father's signal to move. His young brother, Arthur, Jr., sat beside him, shotgun across his saddle, ready to protect his family if necessary.

Dorcas sat in the back of the wagon comforting her daughter, Jane, and her youngest son, Robert. Armstrong had saddled up one of the steeds not needed to pull the wagon and was prepared to ride ahead as a scout. Horace sat atop his old mare beside the wagon. The tension in the air was so thick that even the horses fidgeted and snorted nervously.

As soon as his stepsons arrived, Arthur coolly issued directions for their journey.

"Alright, now. We need to stay calm but alert. The chief told me that most of the troubles are still north and west of here and that the road to Carlisle was clear, last that he heard. Still, we shouldn't tarry or let our guard down. Now, me and Armstrong will ride ahead just a few yards so that we can lookout for trouble before you all ride into it. You follow behind us, but stay within sight. Henry bring your wagon up to the front. Thomas, you change places with Arthur, Jr., so there's a grown man in that wagon, too, then bring that wagon in last. Dorcas, you and the little ones keep a sharp eye out for trouble coming up behind us." Dorcas not only had a sharp eye but was also an expert shot, making her the most capable person in the family to guard the rear.

"Where do you want me, Arthur," asked Horace.

"Horace, I'd much appreciate it if you'd come up here and ride close in front of the lead wagon."

"I'll be happy to."

"Let's all stay as quiet as possible, so we don't draw attention to ourselves and so we can hear if any trouble is coming our way."

The rest of the party all nodded in anxious acknowledgment and agreement. Dorcas settled her young children in the middle of the wagon and took up her post in a corner at the back. She leaned against the sideboard, stretched her long legs out in front of her and turned her face to the trail behind them. A shotgun lay across her legs and her finger and thumb danced around the trigger, ready for action should danger arise. Kilkenny, with his protective instincts piqued, sat in the opposite corner of the wagon, keeping vigil along with his mistress.

Arthur gave the signal and the horses moved forward on the dusty path. Dorcas and her children watched as their beloved home slowly faded from view.

The exodus out of the valley was a tense one. They rode along silently and swiftly, as Arthur had directed. Even the animals walked along without making a sound, seemingly sensing the danger. After the sun went down, the full moon lit the path, allowing them to travel later into the night than most other night skies would have allowed.

The small wagon train stopped for a few hours just after midnight to allow the riders and the horses to rest. They slept in shifts with half of the group sleeping while the other half kept watch. Those who slept, slept only lightly. They did not rest easy until they were out of the valley and Carlisle was within easy reach, nearly two days after their journey had begun.

The entire Buchanan clan, including the newlyweds, moved back into the two-story house on corner of Bedford and High Streets in Carlisle. It was nestled between several other similar brick homes in the center of town, just steps away from the town square. Arthur and Dorcas had lived there and helped William run the tavern before they'd gone to Kish Valley. When William died, he left his share of the house and everything in it to Arthur. They closed it when they moved to Ohesson but they hadn't yet let it out or sold it. Arthur knew that there was a strong chance that they might need to come back to it in times of danger. His intuition had paid off.

The house was still comfortably furnished enough to serve as a home and a tavern. Arthur and Dorcas had taken only their own furnishings with them to Ohesson, intending to eventually sell William's things at a later date, when they were confident that they would not need them further. Dorcas was thankful that they returned to a house complete with tables, chairs and beds. All that they'd been able to take during their hasty escape from the house on the creek were some clothes and a few light provisions.

The tavern dishes were covered in dust but still lined up neatly on the shelf. Mash tubs and a master pot sat at the ready in the back room, as well. The Buchanan family would be able to reopen the tavern and get to making a living again in short order.

The day after their arrival in Carlisle, Arthur went to the Justices of Cumberland County and asked for a renewal of his previous tavern license. His petition was short and to the point:

> *Most humbly showeth that your petitioner as well known to your Honors was drove to this town by*

the savage cruelties with loss of his total effects. He then flying with his family for the preservation of their lives, and rendered unable to support his numerous family without falling into some way of business for their support, etc.

Your petitioner therefore most humbly prays that your Honors will be pleased to consider the premises and the condition of his poor family, and that you will be pleased to grant him a license to retail beer and cider, and your petitioner in duty bond shall ever pray. Arthur Buchanan

Arthur was granted his license on the spot, and he immediately took his Henry and Thomas with him to Lancaster to buy liquor to sell until the first batches he made fermented enough to be served. Arthur didn't like to sell alcohol that he hadn't made himself but, given the circumstances, he really had no choice in the matter.

William and Robert settled animals in the stable out back, while Sarah and Elizabeth opened and cleaned out the house. As the fresh air blew through the open windows, they cleaned the serving room to ready the tavern for business. They stowed the meager belongings they'd brought with them, getting the upstairs room in decent living condition for the family.

Dorcas, Jane and Robert visited the market on the square to get the makings for the food to be cooked and served to their family, as well as the first customers who would soon be crossing their threshold. As soon as word got out that they were back in town, the Buchanans could expect to once again serve a great many customers. By the time Dorcas and the children arrived at the market, the word was already out that Arthur had appealed for and received a new tavern license.

Dorcas told every trader she dealt with, along with every person she met on the street that they were open for business, effective immediately. Their friends, neighbors and former customers were unanimously pleased to see the Buchanans back in Carlisle. Dorcas was an accomplished cook and Arthur was a gregarious barkeep. The food was good and the atmosphere even better, and their establishment was beloved by the citizens of Carlisle. It didn't take long for the tavern to regain its status as the best tavern in town.

The Buchanan clan wasn't the only one to flee the countryside to return to the protection of civilization. Families on the run rolled wagons into town at a steady pace for two solid weeks. With them, they brought fresh news of the attacks in the wilderness. As far as anyone could tell, most of the settlers who had received warning got out before their homes were targeted.

As was to be expected, most of the survivors eventually came to Buchanan's Tavern to learn the fate of their friends and former neighbors. They came seeking solace and, in learning that most of their cherished friends and acquaintances had successfully escaped to the security of Carlisle, there they found it.

Late one quiet afternoon, in the lull between the noon meal and the evening one, the door swung open and in came a slightly chubby man with thick, red curls and an equally thick, red beard. Blue eyes shone out of the red brush that encircled his face.

"Why, Bill Elliott! Does my soul good to see you're still standing. How are you?"

"I'm none the worse for wear, Arthur. Yourself?"

"We're all settling in comfortably here. When did you get into town?"

"Late last night. Had a narrow escape from my place up in the mountains. My neighbor, Sam Patterson, was out hunting when the Indians got to his place. When he was coming back, he saw from a way off what they were doing at his place and he, being the smart fellow that he is, came running straight to my place. We high-tailed it out of there together, riding as fast as we could until we saw the lights of Carlisle. Never been so glad to see any town in all my life."

"I'm glad to see that you made it out in one piece. It's a good thing you hadn't moved your wife and children out there from Boston yet."

"Don't I know it! Arthur, do you happen to know who else made it out unharmed and who might not have?"

"From what I hear tell, most all the settlers made it out thanks to good warning from my friend, Logan, and the other friendly tribes."

"Ah, that's good to hear. Though did you the news about Fort Granville? There's no good news there."

"I heard it was attacked but nobody I've talked to knows yet what happened. Since you're the latest one in, you probably know more about it than anybody else around here."

"Aye, I do. Unfortunately, the fort is gone now."

"Gone? Completely gone?"

"Unfortunately, yes. Burned clean to the ground."

"That's a shame. We just finished building that place not all that long ago."

"Ah, I forgot that you and your boys helped to build it. It was awfully close to your place, wasn't it?"

"Sure was. West of us by about a mile. Me, Henry, Thomas, Armstrong, Arthur and William all helped George Croghan build it. Is there anything left of it?"

"Sad to say, but it's nothing but ashes and memories now."

"How in the world did they get into the fort? I'd have thought it was impregnable. It was built strong and had plenty of soldiers there to protect it. What happened to the people in the fort?"

"Well, for one thing, it's not just the Indians doing these attacks. Some of them banded up with the French to work against the English settlers. Between them, they have quite the supply of guns and ammunition. I heard tell that Captain Ward took a bunch of his fellas out of the fort and over to Shearman's Valley to protect the harvesters.

When he did, that's when the French and Indians went after that fort. Of course, even if Ward and his men had been there, word had it that they were pretty low on ammunition. I'm not sure they could have fended them off anyway. It was a pretty big troop, about a hundred of them, all told."

Speechless, Arthur could only shake his head in sorrow.

"That's a shame. What about my place? Do you know anything of it?"

"I can't rightly say. No one spoke of it to me. I hate to tell you, but word has it that Captain Jacobs led that attack. Sounded like he went plumb mad one day. He burned down his own house and those of all his kin, and then they just up and left. Went west, I suppose. That's the direction most of the angry ones run off to these days."

Arthur was devastated to once again hear that Captain Jacobs was at the heart of it all. He'd dined at the Buchanan table on many an occasion and Arthur once considered him to be a close friend. War could take a terrible toll on kinship and friendship alike.

"Killed Edward Armstrong. Wasn't he kin to your misses?"

"Oh, he sure was. We hadn't had word of that yet. He was distant kin to me, too, on my mother's side. Such a terrible loss. Such a good man. What else do you know? Was anyone else killed at the fort?"

"I don't know, for sure. They say a bunch of the folks surrendered. There were about two dozen soldiers, a couple of women and some children. I heard that the French officer took them off to Kittanning while Jacobs stayed around and set fire to the place."

"What happened to them after they got them to Kittanning?"

"I don't know. No one I've talked to does. There's no word on them yet."

"Well, I guess we just have to be grateful that the rest of us all got out while we could. Lord only knows what we'll find when we go back - if we ever get to go back. I had a pretty nice place going there and it vexes me to think that we might never get back there."

"I heard that the attackers robbed and burned some places to the ground but left others untouched. Maybe it was spared."

"If Jacobs was so angry that he destroyed his own village and moved his people, there's no telling what he would do. I do hope my place was spared, though. Chief Logan told me that he'd try to protect it by telling them it belonged to him now. I don't know for sure if that would keep it protected or not. Time will tell, I reckon." Worry creased Arthur's face.

The French and Indian alliance continued their brutal attacks on settlements in the area throughout the summer and on into the fall. News came to the tavern on a daily basis. It didn't take long for another visitor to the tavern to bring the latest news of the Fort Granville hostages. Dorcas was lighting a fire in the hearth when she heard the door open and the floorboards behind her creak.

"Good day to you, my fair Mrs. Buchanan," cooed a familiar voice. Dorcas turned to find her favorite cousin standing before her.

"Oh, Harmon! It's so good to see your face," she beamed as she ran to greet him. "What brings you all the way over here from Lancaster?"

"Well, I'm moving my home and my shop over here, so I can be closer to you and the boys. I heard you were back in Carlisle now and I'm looking to make a fresh start. I've been out of sorts ever since I lost my Mary. Everybody else moved out this way, so I thought I might as well seek my fortune here, too."

"I'm so pleased to hear that, Harmon. I'm sure that Arthur will be glad of it, too. The whole family will be. Do you have a place in mind yet?"

"I already found a place right at the end of High Street that would be a good spot for me to set up a shop."

"What's this I hear? We're to have a harness maker and saddler handy right down the street," Arthur queried as he came in from the back storeroom.

"You certainly are. Fella said I could have it starting the first of the month."

"You'll be staying here with us until then, of course," exclaimed Dorcas.

"If you have the room. I don't want to impose."

"You'll be no trouble at all. Matter of fact, we might put you to work while you're here," she said with a sly grin on her face. "Make you earn your keep."

"That's good news indeed," exclaimed Arthur as he smiled and shook Harmon's hand. "Come sit, have a drink and let's catch up before that woman tries to put a broom in your hand."

"My mother always told me that the devil finds work for idle hands to do," Dorcas quipped.

"Then let's put our hands to work with these," said Arthur as he poured three tankards of cider and the three took seats around the table.

"I have to say, I was mighty worried about you. I heard tell of all kinds of atrocious things going on over in that valley, up around your old place."

"That's why we're sitting here instead of over there. Plenty of folks got out before all the trouble began but I don't know about how our place or the boys' cabins fared. Did you hear they burned down Fort Granville?"

"I heard that straight from the horse's mouth. John wrote me a letter telling me all about it. He's Lieutenant Colonel Armstrong now, you know. He said he organized 300 men from Fort Shirley and led a raid on that Lenape village of Kittanning. He'd been told that was where the women and children from Granville were taken. They'd killed his brother Edward and he was determined to avenge his brother's' death, as well to rescue those women and children that had been taken."

"Tell us the whole story from the beginning and don't leave one thing out," begged Dorcas.

"It was an early dawn raid, round about September 8, as John told it. Some of those native women and children got away as soon as the fighting started, but their men stayed behind to fight. That's one thing about those Lenape, they sure are courageous people. They'll stand their ground and fight rather than just give it up, even when they are outnumbered."

"But what of the battle? What was the outcome?"

"According to John, it was a complete success. Not a warrior or a wigwam was left standing."

"Not a one?"

"Not a one. Some of them had cabins and they were all burned up, too. He said they probably killed about three dozen of their warriors. John went after the chief himself, that Captain Jacobs fella that used to come to your place."

"Ohh," moaned Arthur, leaning back in his chair and closing his eyes.

"They said that he and his family tried to take a stand in their cabin, but they were outnumbered. Some soldiers set fire to the cabin and chased the family out in the open. Soon as they stepped out the door, the soldiers shot and killed the Chief, his wife and his son before they took three steps." Dorcas reached over to put her hand on Arthur's. It was clear that this story was upsetting him.

"It's a terrible shame that whole families are dying together in this mess. I met his wife a time or two and she seemed to me to be a kind and decent woman," exclaimed Dorcas.

Arthur swallowed hard at the thought of Jacob's family being gunned down. Even though Jacobs had done some unforgivable things as of late, Arthur was brokenhearted at the thought of what had happened to him and his family. He sat for a while, carefully considering his next words.

"These are terrible times. Jacobs was once a true friend to me but the French turned his head and convinced him to side with them in chasing the English settlers out of the valley. I am sad to hear of his death. But . . . I suppose . . . it was inevitable."

"There is some good news in this story that might lift your spirits: The soldiers were able to find the Granville hostages and take them to safety."

"That is good news," Dorcas chimed in. She patted her husband's back with sympathetic affection. She was well aware of how fond her husband had once been of Jacobs and how he must be grieved by this unfortunate turn of events. She was just as aggrieved but her pain was less personal. She wasn't close to the family but her heart ached at the loss of any family, regardless of the color of their skin or their uniform.

The unfortunate truth was that violence was being perpetrated by many and suffered by all. Farmers plowing their fields were murdered by marauding tribes. Innocent tribal women and young children were slaughtered in their homes when their men left them alone to go hunting. Forts were attacked when soldiers ventured out to protect nearby farmers. Cabins were burned regardless of whether they were occupied. No life was respected. Men, women and children of all ages perished.

Arthur Buchanan had always been a peace-loving man and a friend to all. He had a difficult time understanding and accepting the recent division between men who had once gathered in his tavern as one community. Nowadays, men who had once honored each other at his tables were out there killing each other and each other's families in the wilderness. Nothing in his world made any sense at all anymore.

Chapter Nine
1760

"What are you doing? Are you alright," Dorcas asked Arthur. He had been tossing and turning for the past two hours and now he was getting out of bed in the middle of the night, something he'd never done before unless there was trouble about.

"My stomach is churning on me. Think I'll get up and go sit by the fire for a while. Maybe put a little bread in my stomach to settle it."

"Do you want me to come with you? Can I do anything? Maybe make you some peppermint tea? It's good for the stomach, you know."

"Nah. Don't trouble yourself. I'll be right as rain come morning. I just want to get out of this bed and stop this tossing and turning. You go back to sleep now."

"If you're sure. You just holler if you need me."

"I'm sure. You just close your eyes and don't worry another minute about me. This will all pass before the sun comes up."

Dorcas couldn't help but worry about her husband. She was painfully aware that this town life didn't suit him at all. They'd been in Carlisle for about four years now and he resented it more with each passing day. They were quite comfortable and felt safe as they could be in these times, but neither was particularly happy with their living situation. Their hearts and their dreams for the future belonged to the place over on Kish Creek.

Arthur had been slowing down some lately and Dorcas noticed that his color seemed somehow off in recent days. His skin had taken on an odd grayish cast, and he'd lost the usual twinkle in his eyes. A bad fever going around Carlisle in recent weeks and she suspected that he might be coming down with it. She tried to go back to sleep, as her husband suggested, but her worry now left her tossing and turning in his place. She made up her mind that in the morning they would fetch the doctor and see if something could be done to return her man to his normal vigorous state. Surely some sort of tonic could be had that would improve his state.

Three of the wee hours passed before Dorcas could stand it no more. If she couldn't sleep, she would get up and make the most of her day. She arose as if it were dawn, washed her face, put on her dress and pinned up her hair.

She tiptoed down the stairs to the front room to find Arthur asleep at a table in front of the fireplace. A water-filled pewter tankard and a breadcrumb covered plate was pushed across the table in front of him. He'd fallen asleep with his head resting on his arms, his face turned toward the fire.

Dorcas went to him and gently laid her hand on his shoulder.

"Arthur, why don't you go back upstairs and try to sleep in the bed. You'll put a crick in your neck sleeping like that."

Arthur did not stir.

"Arthur?" Dorcas stepped around to look at his face. She gasped when she saw that his eyes were open but unseeing. She touched his hand and found that it was cold. The love of her life had slipped away in the middle of the night.

"No," she whispered. "No, no, no." Tears filled her eyes as she turned away from the sight of her departed husband. "Oh, my love." She put her hand on the mantle to steel herself and took several deep breaths. Surely this couldn't really be happening now. Death was inevitable but Dorcas had always assumed that they would have many good years ahead of them. She was not ready for this. Not yet.

She pulled up a chair next to her husband, wrapped her arm around his shoulders, sobbing alone until the early morning light began to lighten the room and she was able to compose herself enough to do what she had to do. She would have to wake the rest of the family to give them the unfortunate news. She didn't want them ambling downstairs to find him like this with no warning.

There were things that had to be done and Dorcas was determined to remain calm and gather her strength in order to for them to be done properly. She could not allow herself to fall apart in front of her loved ones. Her family would need her strength now more than ever. The only question was, how she might find that essential strength when she felt that every piece of it left with her beloved Arthur.

She looked at the mantel clock and, as her first ritual act of mourning, stood up and stopped the hands, marking the hour of Arthur's passing, or at least her knowledge and acceptance of it. She gently closed his eyes one last time. She placed a loving hand on her husband and whispered a brief prayer for his soul before going upstairs to wake her family to deliver the news. She shuddered with grief and struggled to remain calm as she climbed the stairs to the bedrooms where they were sleeping.

When the everyone was awake and the devasting truth revealed to all, a flurry of activity followed an initial period of shock. Dorcas, always the great general, directed it all. She sent Henry to fetch the undertaker and the preacher, then issued orders for the remaining members of the family.

The front room of the tavern was swept and rearranged so that Arthur could be laid out there. It only made sense to lay him out in the room where he'd entertained nearly every soul in town. It would be fitting to say their good-byes to him in this very room. When the undertaker came, Arthur's sons and step-sons helped to dress their father in his Sunday best. Sarah and Elizabeth took control of the kitchen and fixed breakfast for the family even though no one really wanted to eat. Dorcas insisted that they put something in their stomachs, even if they didn't feel like it. They would need their strength for everything they would be enduring for the next few days. They obeyed their mother's orders and forced down bits of food, though it was the last thing that any of them wanted to do.

While the men were preparing Arthur for the showing, Jane and Dorcas walked down the street to Mrs. Hall's shop to buy mourning ribbon and black bunting cloth. The house must be shown to be in mourning as soon as possible so that customers would not burst in expecting to be served and instead being horrified to find Arthur laid out there.

When they returned to the house, the mother and daughter immediately draped the front door and the mirror with the black bunting. The shutters were closed and tied with black ribbon. They worked together with very few words between them. There was much to be said but neither one could find the right words to say to the other. When the draping was done, they went outside and cut every bloom from the garden at the back of the house, and filled vases and pitchers of water with as many flowers as they could to put around the front room.

Once the house was once again neat and tidy, Dorcas returned to the upstairs bedroom. She opened the lid of the cedar chest and pulled out the mourning dress and the matching black lace cap that she'd worn to her mother's funeral not all that long ago. She would give Arthur's mourning suit to William, who'd recently come to nearly the right size for it and William's would be passed down to Robert. The rest of them could all still wear their mourning clothes from their grandmother's funeral.

It had been a mournful year for the extended Buchanan family. First, they'd lost Dorcas's mother. Then in March, they buried Arthur's Aunt Jeanne, widow of his Uncle Robert. No less than a dozen Buchanan and Armstrong cousins had been lost in the skirmishes. And now, Arthur.

Death and mourning had become a way of life for the entire family. No one embraced death, but they were used to it visiting its sorrows upon them on a too frequent basis.

Dorcas shook out the dresses, pants and jackets, brushed them off and called everyone up to fetch what they would be wearing. She'd never imagined that any of them would need mourning clothes again so soon, and certainly not for their own father's funeral. Not this soon, anyway.

The house was solemn but busy over the next two days. It seemed like the door would barely close behind one visitor before another visitor would open it and follow them in. The majority of Carlisle's citizens came to honor the beloved tavernkeeper, and to comfort his widow and children. Sympathies and support were offered in hushed tones. The solemnity was a disturbing contrast to the laughter that usually resonated off those walls. The tavern felt somewhat strange and surreal to Dorcas. Her own body felt strange. She walked around in a fog as the townspeople came and went.

On the day of his burial, a large crowd of family, friends and neighbors gathered at the tavern just after midday to honor Arthur Buchanan, Sr. one last time. Late in the afternoon, as the shadows grew long, the minister from the Carlisle Presbyterian church, pulled Dorcas aside.

"Dorcas, it's time," he murmured quietly.

Dorcas cast a long, sorrowful glance at her husband's body.

"I suppose so," she sighed. The harsh reality of it all was starting to break through and sink into her brain. She gathered her children around her husband's coffin for a final goodbye.

Dorcas was overcome with grief with the realization that she would never again gaze upon her beloved's face. Her heart and mind couldn't quite grasp the fact that her dear husband, her cherished companion, was really gone. Flanked by her children, she rested her hand on his still arm and bent to kiss his cheek. The children all took their turns saying a respectful and loving goodbye before the undertaker placed the lid on the coffin.

Dorcas's sons served as pallbearers. They lifted the wooden box to their shoulders and began the somber procession from the tavern to the grave. The church bell ringing echoed through the streets of Carlisle while the mourners bowed their heads and trudged down the dusty street to the cemetery.

Dorcas and her children stood stoically by the grave, numbly listening while the minister recited a solemn prayer. When they followed the route back to their home, they did not do so alone. Every mourner who had attended the graveside service escorted them back home.

While the handful of men from the town tended to the final tasks at the cemetery, the neighborhood women had restored the tavern to its original state. Those same women had cooked and baked from the moment that they heard the news and now the serving tables were overlaid with the weight of their efforts. Dorcas unconsciously assumed her role as the tavern mistress, making the rounds and making sure that all of her guests had a plate full of food, but her friends and neighbors quickly put a stop to her efforts.

"Dorcas, let me take care of that and you sit. Let us take care of you for a change," Insisted her closest neighbor, Abigail Holmes.

"Abby, I don't mind, really."

"I insist. No one in your family need be doing any serving or cleaning up. You're in mourning."

"Alright." Even Dorcas knew when it was time to let others take the reins. As her doting friends surrounded her, trying to comfort her, the women working in the kitchen wrung their hands and pondered what the future might hold for Dorcas.

"How is she ever going to get by without him? She has no one to turn to," mused a neighbor woman.

"She still has her boys and their wives with her. Her family stays as thick as can be. I've never seen a family that stays so close."

"And Arthur wasn't the only one running this place. They all ran it well enough whenever he had to go over to Lancaster from time to time."

"That they did."

Out in yard, the men were divided between the sort who sought to profit from her loss and the second sort who sought to protect her from the first sort.

"I wonder if Dorcas will sell now that her husband is gone," queried Simon, an overly ambitious townsman. It was common knowledge about town that the Buchanans had prospered here and he was looking at the tavern with fresh eyes. He was well-acquainted with the Buchanans but no one would have considered him a friend of theirs. He was not the kind of man anyone would want to call a friend.

Unfortunately, Simon was not the only scoundrel out in that yard thinking about profiting from the Buchanan family loss. There were others present who harbored the same idea, but they were discreet enough to keep their mouths shut, at least for now.

"You just get that idea out of your head right now," barked Horace. "Don't you dare go asking her any such thing."

"If you try it, you'll be run right out of this town, mister," scolded Bill Elliott. "I bet you're thinking that she'll be foolish and sell the place cheap. We won't let you take advantage of her that way." In truth, that was exactly what Simon was thinking, that she'd be overcome with grief and so worried about the future that she'd take the first paltry offer that came along.

"Now gentlemen, there's no need to get all riled up," said cousin Harmon. "You all know, Dorcas. She might be in mourning, but she's never been helpless a day in her life, and she never will be. If Simon so much as hinted to her that he was interested in the place, she'd grab him by the seat of his britches, throw him out on the street and let it be known that he'd better never darken her doorstep again. God put red hair on that woman to serve as warning to others."

The men gathered in the yard laughed out loud, even the ones who had earlier been contemplating how they might work Dorcas to their benefit. They were quickly reconsidered those earlier ideas.

A great many of the visitors stayed until well after dark. As the evening fire died down, the women cleaned the dishes, while the men put the chairs back in place. Someone stoked the fire so that the family wouldn't have to tend to it before they turned in. When the last visitor had gone, save her cousin Harmon, Dorcas seemed to regain some semblance of awareness.

"Now Dorkey," he said as her patted her hand. "Don't you be afraid to call on me any time that you need me. I got no one but myself to take care of. I'd be honored to come help you out whenever you need me."

"Thank you, Harmon. I appreciate that. I have my family to help me out here, too. Our children are grown, or nearly so, and they'll be a good comfort and plenty of help to me. I am greatly blessed when it comes to family. And I count you as one of my many blessings, dear cousin."

"And I you, my dear. You'll need and want to take some time to mourn the loss of your husband, won't you?"

"I will most certainly mourn him, more than you can ever know, but I don't have the luxury of indulging in it to excess. I can't sit back mourn for a full year like a year like some city women do. I need to get back to running this place and bringing in what we need to survive. Our whole family worked hard to build this place and we've been pretty successful. I'll not let that all wash away in a sea of useless tears."

Chapter Ten

Early the next morning, Dorcas sat her sons, daughters-in-law and daughter down at the family table in the kitchen to talk things out over breakfast. She was determined to exemplify strength and courage to her children. Deep in her heart, what she really wanted to do was to crawl into bed and not resurface for several days, if ever.

Nevertheless, Dorcas could not and would not fail her family at this desperate time when they were relying on her unfailing strength. Putting on a strong façade when she'd just buried her beloved Arthur, was one of the greatest feats of her life. She selflessly forfeited her own grief for what she perceived to be the betterment of her family. They might all be grown or nearly grown, but they still needed their mother's comfort. Arthur had been the rock that they had all leaned on. He was the true bedrock of the family. She was concerned about how they would all fare with him gone. She'd seen other families come unglued and start fighting or even worse, drifting apart, when one of the parents passed on. She would not let that happen to her family.

"Now I want you all to listen to me and heed what I say. As much as each and every one of us loves your father and will miss him dearly, we are still living, and we have to keep things going. We need to remain strong, no matter how hard that may be. We can't let your father down by letting all that we built fall to ruin because we are grieving. We have many strong hands and good heads among us. We have each other to lean on. I have no doubt at all that we can keep this place going right, just as your father would have."

They all murmured in agreement.

"Momma, I can help," Jane said, sympathetically patting her mother's hand. "What can I do?"

"Jane, honey, you just carry on as you always have. You have been more help to both me and your father over the past few years than you can ever know."

"I can help, too," declared Robert. He fancied himself to be more of a young man than a young boy. Indeed, his father had always treated him so, assigning him chores that were usually assigned to much older boys, knowing full well that the intelligent and capable young lad could face just about any challenge that his father put before him.

"I know that you can, Robert, and I will be counting on your help." She smiled softy and tousled his hair. "I want you to be my special right-hand man. You stay close by me and I'll let you know what you need to do and when you need to do it." Her heart broke for him, losing his father at his tender age. She would be mindful to keep a special eye on him and see to it that he received all the guidance that a young boy would need. Her older sons would also be a great help in that respect. They were old enough to serve as the father figures he would need in the years to come and, the fact was, they already doted on their youngest brother.

"Armstrong, I will be going to the court tomorrow to file the estate papers. I'd like you to come along with me for that. Two heads are better one and mine is rather fuzzy at the moment. You've always shown a talent for dealing with courts and legal papers."

"I wouldn't dream of letting you go alone, Momma."

"Should we reopen the tavern tomorrow? I can run things while you're gone. I've done it enough in the past," offered Arthur, Jr.

"I think we should wait a while longer. We should take some time to mourn properly. Your father was a great man and it will take some time for us to come to terms with the loss of him. It might well prove harder for you than you can imagine when you're thinking about your father. And, everyone in town knows that we are a house in mourning. No one will come around for a long time for any reason except to pay their condolences. We will leave the front shutters pulled to for one month."

"Ours is not an idle family. What are we going to do in the meantime," asked Armstrong. "I, for one, will be happier if I have something to do rather than just sitting idle all day long. I can't imagine us all just sitting around in mourning for more than just a few days."

"The tavern might not be open but there will plenty things to do in the coming days. We are grieving but the chores to keep the house running still need to be done. Winter will soon be upon us, and we need to prepare. There're logs to be split, vegetables to be harvested and a lot of other chores to tend to. You may find that doing your chores will be considerably more difficult and may take you a lot longer to finish what with the loss of your father laying so heavy on your heart, but don't you worry about that. We will take the time to mourn your father properly. We will do our chores but we will mourn."

Chapter Eleven
1762

The Buchanan family stayed in Carlisle for several years, patiently awaiting the opportunity to return to Ohesson, or whatever was left of it. Before the war and the Indian raids plagued the valley, life by the creek was simpler and much more peaceful than in Carlisle. Dorcas loved the seemingly unlimited potential of living by her beautiful creek without the restraints of living in this crowded, dusty city.

Unfortunately, the Buchanans were forced to patiently bide their time for a while. Arthur's estate was not yet settled and, even though things out in the wilds had settled down somewhat, a few tribes were still raiding settlers' cabins from time-to-time. Dorcas worried that the day might never come when she could sit in the sun by her garden and watch the creek flowing by. It also pained her to think that Arthur would again never be able to return to their little piece of paradise. It was his greatest dream unrealized.

Carlisle was a nice enough town, but it was bigger than what suited her. Their city home had a dirty, dusty street running within a few inches of the front door, not a cool, flowing creek. In

Carlisle, she saw horses and wagons and dozens of busy people rushing by all day long. She never once saw a deer or an elk from her Carlisle door as she did her Ohesson door. In Carlisle, she rarely saw even small creatures like rabbits or squirrels in the yard.

Dorcas resented the fact that she was more reliant on other people in town than she was by the creek. She had to buy vegetables from local merchants because she couldn't grow enough in her small plot to feed her family and keep the tavern going. She also had to buy eggs because she couldn't keep enough hens to feed her customers. She often bemoaned the fact that her Carlisle home didn't allow her enough space to keep a few sheep. The past four generations of Armstrongs had all kept sheep and it just felt strange to her not to have three or four of the creatures roaming about on her own property.

As a cleanly woman, Dorcas hated the constant dust stirred up by passing wagons that blew in over her stoop every time the front door opened. She had to sweep the stoop and the entry to the tavern numerous times each day. She'd rather clean up pieces of mud from the Ohesson woodsmen's boots than constantly be chasing that damnable city dust.

Another unfortunate reality of city life was the ever-present odor of horse manure. It was dropped everywhere up and down the street all day long, and it was rarely, if ever, cleaned up. The smell of it wafting through the door could be overpowering, especially on sultry summer days. Naturally, there was manure to be dealt with over at the creek, too, but folks didn't ride up to the front of the house and let it drop right in front of the door. Out there, folks were considerate enough to tie up their horses a reasonable distance from the house.

Carlisle had become a major base of operations for the military and soldiers filled the streets. Dorcas often put up soldiers at the tavern because the reimbursement money was too generous to turn away. Along with the soldiers, the Army brought in an endless parade of military wagons, horses and cannons, stirring up even more dust. Street dust became the bane of her existence in Carlisle. Dust and manure. Dorcas could never understand why folks thought of the city as more civilized than the country when it was so much dirtier and smelly than the country.

However, there were some advantages to being in Carlisle that even Dorcas could appreciate. Along with the soldiers and other newcomers came many fresh prospects. Not only did the soldiers frequent the shops (and the Buchanan tavern) when they weren't in battle but many of their wives came with them, increasing the opportunities for local shopkeepers to enjoy a sizable profit. Settlers from the east were coming to and through Carlisle looking to build new lives and, because of the military presence, Carlisle felt like an uncommonly safe place to be. New shops popped up at every corner of the town, slowly stretching the streets of Carlisle longer and longer as the weeks went by.

The military was encamped just northeast of town and Dorcas found that she enjoyed housing the soldiers who preferred sleeping in wood buildings rather than canvas tents. They found great comfort in her home and she found comfort having them in her home. They kept her up on everything that was going on in and around the camp.

Not only was Dorcas housing several soldiers, but freshly arrived settlers also filled her home until they could build their own places. Dorcas was making more money than she ever thought possible in one lifetime. Even though the entire family privately mourned Arthur, they were well financially. Dorcas was just as good a tavernkeeper as her husband had been and she found some measure of peace in imagining Arthur looking down on her from the heavens and being exceedingly proud of the work that she was doing.

The Buchanans weren't the only family in town experiencing a remarkably lucrative period. Nearly every businessman, and even many soldiers, found ways to capitalize on the abundant opportunities. A few of the more well-to-do officers contracted with suppliers in Lancaster to bring massive amounts of silk and linen fabric, bedding and clothing to town, some of it rather fancy. They brought in household goods, in the form of dishes and cooking pots, that were sorely needed by folks setting up new households. There was money to be made and money to be spent and plenty of things on hand to spend that money on. Carlisle was bustling.

There were some aspects of city life that Dorcas reluctantly admitted that she enjoyed. One thing she enjoyed was the weekly open-air market on the town square. Folks came from miles around to buy, trade and sell all manner of things. Men brought firearms and liquor. Women bartered over spices, sugar, tea, vegetables and eggs. Just about anything that a body could ever want was available on the square in the center of town come Saturday morning. It was always interesting to see the new things that came to town on those market days.

Dorcas also enjoyed the society of several women friends, the one thing she didn't get enough of when they lived by the creek. She appreciated going to a proper church on Sunday morning, rather than having a service in her yard or her home. And she loved getting the news quicker in Carlisle than she ever could in Ohesson. The news in Carlisle was often only hours old. In Ohesson, the news was often weeks old by the time they heard it. Still, Dorcas longed for Ohesson, the one place on earth that she considered to be her true home.

Chapter Twelve

Dorcas was clearing a table of tankards, plates, bones and crumbs left behind by a large party, when the door opened and Horace Watson ambled in.

"Horace, how you keeping this fine day," Dorcas called out cheerily.

"Doing well, Dorkey. Doing well. And yourself?"

"Couldn't be better. You here for supper or did you come just to wet your whistle?"

"To wet my whistle – and to chew your ear for just a bit."

"There's nothing I like better than a long chat with you, my old friend. Sit," she commanded, and he obeyed. "What can I get you this afternoon?"

"Cider, if you please."

"Cider it will be." She walked behind the bar and filled a tankard with for Horace and one for herself, as well. "Got something special on your mind," she asked as she returned to the table and sat down beside him.

"Yes, there most certainly is, Dorcas. And I think it will be of special interest to you, too."

"You have my full attention."

"I heard some fellas talking the other day. They were saying that the troubles around Ohesson are over now and that it looks as though it might be alright to go back. I'm thinking of heading back over that way and see if my old cabin is still standing. I heard that a lot of the old places still are."

"Who'd you hear that from?"

"Angus Fife. You remember him, don't you? He said that he rode over just to have a look around and that some folks are already there. He claims that more are heading out that way. He's all ready to pack up and go first thing tomorrow morning."

"How many folks have gone? Any count?"

"I don't rightly know. He just said folks. So, tell me, Mrs. Buchanan, are you inclined to give it some thought yourself?"

"Horace, you surely know that I am. We all loved living there before the troubles. Ours was the only tavern in those parts. If things stay peaceful, we could build things up like they were before. Folks will be coming through there at a regular pace now, if what Angus says is true. If things really have settled down over there, then there's no reason not to go back. When are you thinking of going, Horace?"

"In a day or so."

"That soon?"

"Well, you know I've got nothing to keep me here, and it's not like it will take me long to pack. When we high-tailed it out of there, all I took was my guns, my horse and the clothes on my back. All I've bought since then is some more clothes. You know that I've been staying over with my cousin, Dave McClain. He and his wife are good folk, but I'd sure like to get back to my own cabin, if it's still there. If not, I'll build another in its place. Miranda is buried there and when my time comes, I'd like to be laid next to her."

"Well now, Horace, don't get into too big of a rush – for either part of that plan. I am as anxious to get back there as you are but I don't think you should go out there alone. Let me talk to my boys. If you could wait just a little longer, we could all go back together and keep an eye out for each other."

"I suppose I could a wait a while longer, but how much of a wait are you thinking about?"

"Not long. You know me. When I make up my mind to do something, I do it. Though, I sure won't pick up and go if the boys don't agree to come along. I don't see how I could. They'd all have to agree because what we do, we do together as a family. I won't force them to go if they're not ready."

"Dorcas, you are blessed to have the family you have. Not all of us have been that blessed."

"Horace, you might not have any family of your own, but you know that we consider you to be an important part of ours. We'd be lost without you."

"Then I am a lucky man, aren't I? There's no family I'd rather be a part of. I feel the same way about all of you."

The door opened again, and Thomas sauntered in.

"Thomas, what do you think? Horace was just telling me that's safe to go back to go back home."

"I'd go for that, if things have settled down over that way." He swung the chair next Horace around backwards to the table and straddled it, resting his hands on the chair's top rail. "Tell me, Horace. Tell me everything you've heard."

"Just that the troubles are over, and folks are heading back that way. I'm going myself real soon."

"You are? When?"

"Well, I was going to go in a day or so, but your mother here has convinced me to wait just a few days."

"Why is that," he asked, casting a raised eyebrow glance at his mother. "Why should Horace hesitate to go back home?"

"You know full well why, you rascal," she laughed, giving his arm a playful tap.

"So are we to pick up and head back north," Thomas asked of his mother.

"I'd like to go, but we need to talk to the rest of the family and make sure that each and every one of them agrees."

"Oh, they'll agree. Carlisle is nice enough, but the country life suited us better. Even old Kilkenny seemed to be happier by the creek than he does here."

"I know it suited me better," agreed Dorcas. "Horace, you might not have to wait too long for that answer after all."

"Good, I'm raring to go."

"Thomas, why don't you see if you can round up your brothers and their wives to meet up after supper and we'll talk it out. Horace, you ought to come, too."

A few hours later, Dorcas sat at the head of the table, like a queen holding court. She'd gathered her entire family around the table. Horace sat by her side, ready to chime in and plead his case.

"You know that Horace came in here today, talking about going back over to the old place. Seems like things have settled down over there and, while nothing is certain, it sounds like it's more peaceful than ever. I'm thinking that it might be time to head back. What do you all think," asked Dorcas with just a hint of a hopeful smile on her face.

"What folks are going back? How many? Did any of our old friends or neighbors go back," asked William.

"A handful, I reckon. I don't know that anyone we know personally has gone back yet," answered Dorcas.

"Some of the soldiers are reporting that a lot of the Indians have pushed pretty far west and out of the area," reported Armstrong.

"And as sad as it is to say it, a great number of the more aggressive ones were killed in battle," said Arthur.

"And some more of the troublesome whites, as well, is what I heard tell. You know that the Indians weren't the only ones stirring things up," argued Thomas.

"How well I know it. We could pack up a few things and give it a go for a while. If all goes well, we can come back and fetch what we want, then sell the rest. If we don't like the feel of it, we can turn tail and run back here real quick," suggested Arthur. "We've done it before and we can do it again, if we have to."

"I'd like to leave Sarah and the baby here until we make sure it is safe," explained Henry.

"Mmm. I don't like the idea of putting the baby through the travel or putting him in harm's way when it's not necessary," agreed Sarah.

"And one other thing to consider is that we don't know if our homes are still standing. They say that a lot of places of been burned clean to ashes. It wouldn't be fitting to take them into the wilderness without knowing that they'd have a real roof over their heads. Henry, you might not like it, but I think you should stay here with Sarah, run the tavern and make sure that the younger ones are looked after, just for a while. It won't hurt to keep the tavern open just in case we have to make a hasty retreat again."

"Well, I'm just as anxious as the rest of you to go, but I do think it right that I stay here with my wife and children. Tom, you ought to leave Elizabeth and your young ones here with me, as well."

"I intend to do just that. I want to go with Momma to watch over her and help get things running again, but I'll rest easier knowing that my wife and children are here with you, out of harm's way."

"How about we load up just one of the wagons, head that way and scout things out. When we know better what the situation is, we can come back and fetch the others and the rest of our belongings," agreed Arthur. "I think we should stay a few weeks and assess the situation carefully before we take the whole clan back over there."

"That sounds like a wise plan," said Dorcas. "What do the rest of you think? Are you ready to take that chance?"

"I say every man and woman in agreement raise their glass," commanded Henry. Every glass around the table was instantly raised.

"That's settled then. When should we go," questioned Arthur.

"Horace here said he was planning on going in just a few days. Now is as good a time as any for me. I'd just as soon get over there and plant a garden as soon as possible because I suspect that we're going back to stay. I need to get things planted either here or there and I'd prefer that it be there."

"I can be ready the day after tomorrow," said Armstrong.

"Margaret and I can be ready just that quick, can't we," answered William.

"We sure can," answered Margaret.

"Well now that we've decided, there's no sense in putting it off," suggested Dorcas.

"Wonderful! Horace, will you be ready to ride when we are," asked Thomas.

"Heck, I'm ready right now," he chuckled. Horace was mighty pleased that he'd be returning to Kish Valley in the company of the Buchanans.

Dorcas kept the tavern open as she packed, loading up things for the trip between waiting on customers who came and went, and instructing Henry on what would need to be done after she and the others left.

"Henry, help me decide what to take this time and what to take later." Every little item required careful consideration.

"Well Momma, you need enough things to get the tavern up and running right again but you won't have very much room in one wagon. You'd better plan on taking at least two wagons. You have enough drivers."

"That's true. You'll need enough to keep this place running right until we decide when or even if we're at the creek permanently, so we don't want to take things you might need here."

"It's rougher and tumble out there in the country than it is here in town. How about we leave the fancier things here, like that Delft punchbowl. Most trappers and farmers don't care about fancy trappings like the townsfolk do," she reasoned.

"There's two of these here tin coffee pots. How about you take one and leave one here."

"That'll do. What else do we have two of that we can split like that?"

"Plenty. We've plates and cups and tankards and such."

"Let's split up the cider and the whiskey, too."

"I think you should take old Bess, too. We can always buy milk here in town but you won't be able to buy it out in the country."

"That's good thinking. Let's look at all the supplies like that, what you could easily buy here but that I won't have access to out there. I will leave you plenty of money to buy what you need."

"Looks to me that you aren't going to be traveling as light as you first thought, after all."

"Does seem that way but we still have to try to pack light. We left most everything there but God only knows if there is anything left of it."

"Is there going to be room in the wagons for everything you need?"

"I don't know. We should take some tables and chairs, too. You're right that we're going to need two wagons for this move."

"You're pretty sure that you're going to stay this time, aren't you, Momma?"

"I'm hoping and I'm praying to God above that we get to stay this time. I'm tired of moving back and forth. You know they say that three removals are as bad as one fire. We've done more than three removals over the past few years. I'm weary of it. I'm ready to reclaim my home and stay there for the rest of my natural born days."

The Buchanan clan spent the next day loading up the wagons with their clothes, food, firewood, furniture and everything else they needed to survive and to run a suitable enough tavern in the wilds. Every member of the family old enough to carry pitched in and helped with the work. They were excited and filled with joy and hope for the future.

"As soon as old Mrs. Allen from across the street looked out her window and saw the Buchanans packing their belongings, word of their departure spread from one end of Carlisle to the other. Neighbors and friends came calling to say their fond good-byes and offer prayers for safe travel.

"Heard you were heading back to Ohesson. We'll be sad to see you go, Mrs. Buchanan," exclaimed their neighbor, John Brown.

"You could come out that way yourself, John. You're always talking about moving on to greener pastures. There's plenty of opportunity out there."

"I'll think on it but I'll wait and see if you come back with your scalp still attached first," he quipped, boldly echoing what their friends and neighbors were thinking.

The Buchanans were understandably nervous as they guided the wagons through the pass back to the valley but the journey was a peaceful one. They saw no signs of trouble, past or present, as they traveled the old, familiar roads through the countryside.

As the wagons neared the bend in the road leading up to the old house, Dorcas subconsciously held her breath. She was guiding the team pulling the lead wagon, Jane sitting at her side. Each member of the family was holding their breath, just as Dorcas was. When they rounded the bend, there was a loud, collective sigh of relief.

"It's still there," she sighed softly, tears glistening in her eyes. The setting sun was shining on the house like beam of hope and the promise of good things to come. Not only was the house still there but the shutters were still present over the windows and pulled shut, as was the front door. Chief Logan had protected it, just as he had promised Arthur, Sr., so many years ago. Dorcas would be forever grateful for that protection. She smiled and whispered, "Thank you, Logan, wherever you are."

"At least it's still standing, though it's hard telling what it's like inside. At least we can sleep indoors with a roof over our heads tonight and that's enough to make me happy for now."

They tentatively climbed down from the wagons as the riders dismounted from their horses. Dorcas walked slowly up the three steps to the door and stood for a moment with her left hand on the doorlatch. She placed her right hand on the door frame and said a little prayer before she opened the door to face whatever she must face on the other side.

She went in and everyone else timidly followed her, dreading what they might find. The last rays of sunlight were fading, and the room was dim, but they could see well enough. The house had been raided and everything but the cobwebs had been stolen.

"It may be empty but it looks to be in good shape. Logan did right by us. He really did. I don't see where we need to fix anything at all. A good sweeping and airing out is all it needs."

"And some furniture."

"That certainly would make it more comfortable, wouldn't it?"

"Just see to it that you bring in the chairs last, though. I don't want you boys sitting about when there's work to be done," Dorcas joked.

Chapter Thirteen

Everyone slept soundly through the night, overjoyed to be back in the old Buchanan homestead. As usual, Dorcas was the first one up in the morning. She stoked the fire for breakfast, fried some sausage and toasted a few slices of bread before she woke the rest of the household. She brewed a large pot of strong coffee, toasted some bread and set out the boiled eggs that had survived the trip in from Carlisle. They'd need a good breakfast in them if they were to get things up and going the way that she intended.

Dorcas climbed the stairs and stood in the central hall, calling out to the rooms where most of her brood lay sleeping soundly.

"You all get up and get moving now," she called out. "There's plenty of work to be done today and the sun will be up soon. None of you will be lying around idle for one more minute and that's for sure."

"And I'm sure you have the work all planned out, Momma," answered Armstrong, sitting on the edge of the bed, pulling his boots on.

"You know that I do at that, young man."

"Where would you like me to start," asked Thomas, standing at the top of the stairs, pulling up his suspenders and getting ready to go down and get to work.

"The first thing that we need to do is stock some more food. Tom and Armstrong, you go out and get us some game. The smokehouse is empty and you two are in charge of filling it back up. We'll be hitting a whole lot of fish until you do. Margaret, I'd like for you to go milk Bess."

"Yes, ma'am," they replied in unison.

"Jane and I will start getting the house in order and get it ready to open for business again. There might not be many folks here now but, as soon as the word gets out that it's safe enough to return, we'll have plenty of visitors. They'll be streaming in through that door before we know it."

"Arthur, you and Horace go over and check on his place. Horace, I don't want you staying over there at night for a while, but you should go check it out and start getting it ready just the same."

"I appreciate that Dorcas," he answered. He truly did appreciate the way that she tended to look out for him. Horace would never worry about being alone in this world as long as the Buchanans were nearby.

"William, you get out there and clean up that garden and get it ready for planting."

"Yes, ma'am."

"I know that it's somewhat late for planting, but we can still get some cabbage, radishes, carrots and such in the ground and have them harvested before winter sets in."

"What do you want me to do, Momma," asked Robert.

"I want you to go fetch us some water from the creek. After that, you go looking for some kindling but don't go too far. You stay in sight of the house. We still don't know quite how things are out there."

"Yes, ma'am."

"While you're down at the creek, see if you can find any mussels. Later on, you and me are going to go catch some fish for our dinner and some mussels would go real good with that fish. Now, we've a busy day ahead of us, so everyone finish up your breakfast and get to it."

Mid-morning found Robert and Dorcas standing knee-deep in the cool creek, about three yards downstream from a large school of bluegill.

"Now, real gentle and real quiet, just slip one hand in the water and face the palm of it open toward the bank of the creek. Spread your fingers just a little." She spoke softly, so as not to disturb the fish.

"Then what?"

"You see those fish heading our way?"

"Uh-huh."

"When one swims up by your hand, wait until he's close enough that you can close your fingers in under him, then grab him and throw him up on the creekbank."

"Just grab him? What if one doesn't swim close enough?"

"Oh, they'll come close enough. We'll just stand here and wait and the whole school will work its way down here in a minute or so. You might have to reach out a little bit, but they'll come by close if you stand real still and don't stir up the mud under your feet. Now mind you, don't close your hand too early or too tight or the fins will poke your hand. Wait till his head is just past your fingers before you close in."

Robert didn't have to wait long before a mature bluegill swam near enough for him to grab. He closed his fingers and cried out laughing, "I got him!"

"Good! Now throw him up there on the bank. We're going to want a basket full of them if we want to make a decent meal for the house full of family that we'll be feeding tonight."

"Why don't we just grab some of those big old catfish? They're a lot bigger."

"You don't ever want to catch a catfish by hand. They'll poke you for sure. And they're too hard to skin. Bluegill are easier to clean and they taste sweeter. Try to stick to those little fellas you see just upstream there. They're big enough to eat but not too big to catch barehanded."

Mother and son filled their big, round basket with more than enough fish for dinner, then filled two buckets with water before heading back up to the cabin. Along the way, they met the successful hunters who returned carrying two furry rabbits, as well as a good-sized turkey. Horace was walking along with them, carrying two large bowls from his old cabin, tucked up under his arms.

"We got out too late in the day for deer, but these fat, lazy fellows will give us a good enough dinner," claimed Armstrong.

"We got us a basket of fish, too," said Dorcas. "Robert did real well for his first time out."

"My old blackberries did really well this year, Dorcas. Look here," said Horace, showing her the bounty he'd collected.

"Where did you find those bowls, Horace?"

"In my cabin. My place didn't get hit hard at all. I've still got pretty much everything I left behind. Granted, there wasn't much there to begin with, but what little bit I had is all still there."

"Glad to hear that. We'll eat good tonight, that's for sure," said Dorcas. "After the work we've done today, you'll all likely overstuff yourselves and then pass out like fat bears."

Thomas and Armstrong set up a butchering table in front of the barn and readied the rabbits and the turkey. Dorcas led Robert to her favorite worktable out behind the kitchen.

"Come along, Robert. I'll show you how your daddy could clean a fish so there's no bones in it. I've taught you how to fish and once I teach you how to prepare a fish, there's no reason you'll ever have to go hungry in your lifetime."

Margaret and Jane had the main room ready by the time the hunters and gathers brought in their bounty. The long table was set and as soon as the food was ready, they crowded in around it. Everyone lingered around the table for several hours after dinner, nibbling on leftovers, telling stories, laughing and congratulating themselves on a right respectable day of work. The house was once again their home.

Dorcas took a long look around the table and thought about how happy Arthur would have been to see this day. He would have settled in his big chair at the end of the table, enthralling them with his own stories of his trapping days and his early years in Ireland. She was quite content with the way things were shaping up, except that she longed for Arthur to be there among them.

"You did good work here today. Tomorrow, let's some of us go over to the other cabins and see how things stand there."

"Are you anxious to kick us out, Momma," asked Thomas.

"Heavens no. I want you all under my roof until I feel like it's alright for you to go back on your own. But, we ought to get over there and see what's left and what'll have to be done to get things in right shape. I'm sure you'll want to get back over there as soon as the time comes."

"I don't know – the eating is pretty good right here," Thomas chuckled as he popped another handful of blackberries into his mouth.

Chapter Fourteen

Over the next several days, Dorcas turned her attention to getting the tavern back to where it was before their previous hasty departure. What they had done thus far would serve the family well enough but they also needed to get ready to serve the customers who would eventually show up. There were dishes and mugs to put out for service and pots and pans to be readied. Chairs and tables would need to be polished to a shine and arranged. Eventually, they would need more tables and chairs. They'd brought a few with them but not enough for the crowds that Dorcas expected in the coming months. She'd put Armstrong to work building some straight plank tables and benches. He was a skilled carpenter and would be able to put them together in due time.

They'd brought enough candles from Carlisle to fill the sconces and tables for a month or two but she'd have to either make more or arrange to have more sent from the city soon. The boys would soon have the smokehouse filled but they needed more supplies than just meat. She'd have to churn some butter and make more soap, soon. The list she kept in her head of chores to do be done went on and on, seemingly without end.

Every one of them would all be working diligently for a long time to come. Her intention was for them to be as self-sufficient as possible as soon as possible.

While Dorcas, Margaret and the younger children organized the household, Thomas, Armstrong and Arthur, Jr., made regular scouting trips out into the wilderness to make sure the valley actually was as secure and peaceful as it appeared to be. They always came back from their scouting trips laden with rabbits, racoons, wolves and deer that would provide both meat for the smokehouse and furs to sell in the months ahead. Dorcas's children did her proud with the way that they all chipped in to get the work done. She teased them about getting their lazy selves to work but there wasn't a single lazy bone among them.

Dorcas had done considerably well carrying on without Arthur, but coming back home and reopening the tavern sharpened the pain of her loss. It broke her heart that he never got to come back to the slice of the heaven on earth that they had created together. She knew that he would much rather have died and been buried here on their homestead than in Carlisle, where he never quite felt at home. However, it was just not to be, and she would have to accept that harsh reality and move on with her life as it was. She prayed to God that when her time came, that it would be right here by the creek. She wanted her body to be laid where her heart dwelt.

In the months to come, a slow but steady stream of settlers flowed into the valley. At first, just like in the early days, the men came in on horseback. They'd ride in groups of four or five for the protection that comes in numbers. Once they re-established their homesteads and determined that the time was right, they'd head back to Carlisle, Lancaster or Philadelphia to gather the rest of their family. When the families came, they rode in caravans, providing some reassurance to the women and children that they were not alone, and to emphasize the fact that where they were going was free from danger.

Those caravans often made their first stop in the valley at *The Bounding Elk*. Dorcas's place was a busy as ever, as a trading post as much as a tavern. Old friends about to embark on the journey would send word ahead that they were coming and ask if they might stay a night or two at the tavern and to ask what supplies from town Dorcas might want them to bring along.

Her most frequent request was for candles. Dorcas could make them, but it made more sense for her to get them from other folks. The tavern needed more candles than most households and those were easy enough for friends to transport from city shops. When folks would arrive at the Buchanan place, they would trade boxes of candles for the things that they weren't able to carry with them on their long journeys. It was an enterprise that served the growing community well.

Once they settled into their homes, some women would bake extra bread or spin extra wool to trade. Some might bring herbs or fresh vegetables from their gardens. Every person was in need of something and every person had something to offer. Everything a body could possibly need or want could be found at the Buchanan place.

One of the greatest needs in the valley, an intangible one, was that of socializing with others. *The Bounding Elk* provided ample opportunity for that, as well. The returning settlers wasted no time in making the tavern the center of town gathering place, as it had been in earlier days. Horace and other bachelors came for meals and ale. Men and women alike came to trade. It seemed as though the front door was constantly opening and closing from the moment the morning sun peeked into the valley from the east until it escaped to the west in the evening.

The French and Indian War was good and over now and many of the local tribes had pushed further west, away from Ohesson. Although, no one called it by its Indian name anymore. Most of the locals started calling it Old Town.

As the valley filled with more and more cabins, several of the women and a few of the men began to yearn for regular church services like the ones that they had enjoyed during their city years. Minerva Wallace and Penelope Singer showed up on laundry day, just as Dorcas was hanging her sheets on the line to dry.

"Hey ho, Dorcas," Minerva called out in a sunny voice, as she strolled down the hill, arm in arm with Penelope.

"Well, hello, ladies," came the equally sunny answer. "How nice to see you both."

"And you, as well," answer Penelope.

"Penelope and I would like to talk to you about something we deem to be of great importance to everyone around these parts."

"I'll be happy to sit and talk to you for a while. Let's go inside and I'll put on some water to boil for tea. Let's go into the kitchen where we can talk away from the customers that are in the front room." The two visitors settled into worn wooden chairs and leaned into the table, anxious to share their idea with their hostess.

"Dorcas, I know you're awfully busy, so I'll get right to it," began Minerva. "We want to hold a regular church service every Sunday morning and we'd like to do it right here at the tavern." Dorcas didn't hesitate to give her answer. Folks needed to go to church regularly but the closest one was clear over in Carlisle. Valley people couldn't travel over the mountains very often merely for church services.

"Ladies, that's a wonderful idea. We're long overdue for some kind of church worship. Yes, we can do it here, every Sunday. When do you want to start?

"Is next Sunday too soon?"

"That's not too soon at all. We've got plenty of space and the chairs all ready. When the weather's nice, we can carry some chairs and benches out into the yard. Who do you have in mind to lead the service and do the preaching?"

"My uncle, Albert Jessop, over in Lancaster is just starting out as a circuit preacher. He told me that he'd be glad to come this way from time to time," volunteered Penelope. "He will be here this coming Sunday."

"We thought we'd ask a few of the more educated men in the valley to fill in when Mr. Jessop can't be here. I can think of three or four who are well-versed in the Bible and who I am sure would be willing and able to do it on a moment's notice."

"And who like to hear themselves talk a little, too," joked Penelope.

"Oh, we do have a few of those kind of men around these parts, don't we," replied Minerva.

"Alright then. It's all settled. I'll put a notice up on the front door and you two tell everyone you know. It's high time we got us a church right here in the valley."

From that day forward, Sunday church services were held in the yard when the weather was good and inside the tavern when it rained or turned too cold. When the congregation grew too big for the tavern, the men made more rough-hewn benches and services were moved to the barn. As time went by, it became a regular habit that the churchgoers tucked baskets of food and jugs of drink in their wagons to share all around when the prayer service was over. Wagons would appear in front of the barn just after first light and would remain there until the shadows grew long. The men would linger in the yard after the prayer service to talk about their crops or hunting or news from the east. Women would pull up chairs in front of the fire to read to each other and to share their communal wisdom on child-rearing, sewing or whatever else came to mind. Children would run and play all up and down the creek, regardless of the weather. The Buchanan place was livelier than ever.

Dorcas reigned as queen of the fireside chats, simply because she knew how to do so many things that many women in the valley did not. She could tell them where they should walk and what areas to avoid. She knew which woman to call as a midwife when a baby was coming and what medicine to give that baby when a fever came. She could make a healing tea using the bark from a sassafras tea to calm a cough and a mint one that would soothe a troubled tummy. She would lead them to the best nut trees and berry patches. It appeared that there was nothing that Dorcas didn't know or couldn't find out.

The neighbor women admired Dorcas and her amazingly independent spirit. They reckoned that if she could survive out in the wilderness without a husband, surely they could survive and thrive there with a husband. They clamored to be around her in hopes of not only capturing some of her indomitable spirit but also to learn all that they could from her.

Most of the local women depended on Dorcas and what she had to offer. She was part hostess, part business woman and, to a notable extent, part community leader. Oftentimes, when their husbands went off on long hunts, they would pack up their children and go to the Buchanan house rather than stay home alone. Whenever one of them was in need of help in any way, they'd run straight to *The Bounding Elk*, knowing that they would find sanctuary there.

Dorcas was opening the tavern early one morning when she saw Nancy Patton hurrying up the footpath, carrying a lidded iron pot.

"Nancy, what brings you out so early on a cold morning like this?"

"Dorcas, could I trouble you for some fire this morning? Mine went out in the night and my Matthew is off on a hunt. I tried starting it up myself but I'm not doing so good with it."

"Of course, you can. Can't have you and those young'uns going cold."

"And they're already hollering for their breakfast. It's mighty hard to cook without fire."

"Never tried it myself but I'm sure you're right," she joked, taking the pot from her neighbor's hands and filling it with embers. "My fire's burning strong, so there's plenty of coals there for you to take."

"Dorcas, I don't know what the women folk around here would do without you."

"Oh, you'd get on just the same. We all depend equally on each other around these parts."

"Well, I want you to know that none of us take you for granted."

"I'm so pleased that I can help."

"Oh, I near forgot – I brought you some of my special herb tea."

"Why thank you, Nancy. You certainly didn't have to do that, but I appreciate it. You make such a wonderful tea. I'll look forward all day long to having a special cup of it later tonight, once my work is done."

The needs of the valley families were endless. Pioneer women had to rely on their neighbors as much as they did their husbands. Doing so was a crucial element of their survival.

Things had certainly changed since Arthur first built the trading post. In the early days, it had been mostly a fur trade made up of nothing but men. Now that families were moving into the area, more and more women were trading. Arthur had traded mostly furs, guns and knives. Nowadays, Dorcas would a wide variety of household goods. Whatever they had to trade they would bring to Dorcas. Whatever they needed they carried away with them.

In the midst of a blustery October afternoon, a breathless, pale, teary woman burst in the door, calling out for Dorcas. She cradled a weeks-old baby in her arms.

"Susannah, what's wrong? You look as though you've seen a ghost."

"Some Indians came and raided my home! They took all my food stores and everything else they could carry. Stephen is over helping with the Patton's barn raising and I didn't know what to do other than run here to you."

"Are you hurt? Is the baby alright?"

"No, they didn't touch us. They weren't violent but they took nigh everything I had, even my brand-new teakettle. They like to scared me to death. I was so 'fraid for my babe. I've heard terrible tales of what some of them do to babies."

"How many of them were there?"

"Three. They were grown but they seemed young. They couldn't have been more than about 14 or 15 years old."

"What few tribes we have around here are friendly and quiet these days. I served a few of their men right here at this table two nights ago. Must be a bunch of ornery boys looking for mischief."

The door flew open again and in flew another harassed, grousing woman.

"I declare! I thought we were safe here," exclaimed the round, old woman. She huffed and puffed as she peeled off her wrap and plopped it down on a small table near the hearth.

"Did those Indians come to your place, too, Ada?"

"They did at that, and they took everything but my furniture. They even took my old broom. What in the world would they want with my old broom?"

"I'd venture a guess that they heard most of our men are over helping with the Pattons' barn and they thought they'd take advantage of us women being alone to have some fun. I'm sure their fathers would tan their hides if they knew what they were up to."

"I'd like to tan their hides myself. They were laughing and playing the whole time they were robbing me."

"Did they have weapons? Were they on foot or horseback?"

"They had some skinning knives in sheaths that I think that they just stole from someone else, but no guns or bows. Came down the creek in a canoe and, from what I saw as they were leaving, they were robbing cabins all along the creek. They're probably heading this way right now."

"Well good, then."

"Good? Are you crazy? Are you looking for trouble?"

"I'm looking to stop trouble," she declared as she stomped over to the hearth and grabbed the old shotgun from its resting place over the mantle.

"What are you going to do, Dorcas," asked Ada.

"I'm going to go stop those young rascals before they bother any more of our women."

"Shouldn't you wait till your sons get back from the Patton place?"

"No need for that."

"Lord have mercy, Dorcas. Don't you go getting yourself hurt."

"Neither one of you saw any guns with them, right?" The women shook their heads. "And you said they were mere lads, right?"

"Seemed to be," answered Ada.

"Then they have more to be scared of than I do."

"Oh, please be careful, girl," she counseled.

"I really don't think there's any danger to be had from these boys but I won't let this foolishness continue. I'm just not having it. They're mere young bucks trying to act like tough, grown men. You all sit right here, and I'll be back shortly."

"Don't you want one of us to come with you," asked Susannah.

"No. They need to know that I mean business and they know that they already scared you two. My shotgun and temper will make it clear that they can't scare me. They'll know that I mean serious business."

She stormed out the door and headed up the creek along the bank. Her temper was up. She had no patience for the kind of sport these boys were indulging in and she would put a quick stop to it. Life here was difficult enough without this kind of foolishness adding to their difficulties.

Dorcas found the three young marauders sitting on the bank, laughing and eating the food they'd stolen from her neighbors' tables. She was inwardly relieved that she recognized each one of them.

They jumped up in shock, dropping the food from their hands, when they saw Dorcas storming towards them, gun in hand. Her determined gait made it clear that she was not a woman to be toyed with.

"You there," she bellowed. "What do you think you're doing, taking food and such from innocent women and children? You ought to be ashamed of yourselves."

They stood stock-still in complete awe. They'd never seen a white woman as bold as this one. They eyed the gun, wondering if she intended to use it. This woman with hair the color of fire, and with just as bright a fire in her jade green eyes, stood before them, looking as angry as a wounded bear. They could see that she was fearless and would likely give them an awful fight. For all they knew, she might be crazy and ready to shoot. Mrs. Buchanan had a reputation of being a force to be reckoned with and they didn't fancy a reckoning.

"I know who you all are and I know who your fathers are, too. They would be ashamed each one of you."

They hung their heads in disgrace and looked at their feet. They were relieved that she likely wouldn't shoot them but she certainly was going to make them regret their afternoon misadventures. They'd pay dearly if she did go to their fathers and report what they had done.

"Don't just stand there. You take everything you stole and put it out there on the bank and leave it for the rightful owners to reclaim."

They swiftly and silently obeyed this wild woman. They'd gone off in search of fun, not trouble – and certainly not trouble like this.

"Now, you get back in that canoe of yours and go back home where you all belong. Don't you come this way looking for trouble no more. We won't stand for it. We don't come cause trouble for you and we aren't going to let you cause trouble for us, either. Get now! Get on home!"

The embarrassed young men dumped their plunder on the bank and hastily climbed into the canoe. They pushed away, not daring to so much as glance back in her direction. She turned and stared at them angrily until they paddled well past her place, then made her way back home.

"Well, now that's done," Dorcas announced as she returned. "Your things are laying out there on the bank. Let's go get my garden cart and load it up to take back where it belongs. They ate some of the food but I think most everything else is still there and in one piece."

"Dorcas, you could have got yourself killed," exclaimed young Susannah.

"I wouldn't have gone out there if I thought that was true. When I walked up on them, I could see they weren't any older than my Jane. And I recognized them. I told them that I knew their papas and I do. They are all good men and they would want no part of this kind of thing."

"Dorcas, you are the bravest woman I know."

"Nah, not at all. There's nothing brave about straightening out wayward children."

"Those children were near grown men. They could have hurt you."

"I really don't think they would have. I knew I could shame them into doing the right thing. They come from civilized families who hold them to better behavior than that."

The next morning, Thomas came in with a serious, deeply concerned expression on his face.

"Mamma, what's this I hear you took on some Indians at the creek yesterday?"

"Oh, I wasn't in any danger. They were just mean kids. It wasn't like they were full-grown warriors."

"That may be the case this time, but you've got to be more careful. You can't be taking risks like that. You might think you're unbeatable but you're not."

"Don't make a mountain out of molehill, son."

"This might be a mountain that you're trying to make into a molehill. You might know the locals but what if some outsiders come down that creek one day? What if they aren't ornery kids but grown, dangerous men?"

"Then I'll deal with that if and when it happens. Meantime, we've got plenty of work to do around here," she declared dismissively. "I'm busy and you should be, too. You just go tend to your own work and leave me be."

Chapter Fifteen

By Christmas of 1862, it was determined that, come February of the next year, Jane would marry the respectable Mr. Charles Magill who lived over in Bedford County. Dorcas had a penchant for doing things up right, regardless of their circumstances, and she was determined that her only daughter's wedding would be done up right with no slip-ups or omissions whatsoever. The Magills and the Buchanans were both respected, upright families and Jane's wedding would reflect that undisputable fact.

Dorcas didn't worry about any trouble visiting their doorstep during the wedding. So many folks were coming for the ceremony that Old Town would more closely resemble a large eastern town rather a small, frontier settlement. Only a fool would try to attack such a large gathering of able-bodied pioneers. She wouldn't let Thomas's admonitions worry her. He was right that something unfortunate could happen at any time, but she wouldn't let it lay heavy on her mind during the wedding.

The wedding ceremony and the reception would both be held at the tavern, as it was the only suitable building in the valley. Folks would be coming from all around. The Magill clan and several others would arrive the day before the wedding, and many would stay for at least two days afterward. Henry would be bringing the family from Carlisle, and they would stay for several days before returning to the security of Carlisle. The tavern and the surrounding Buchanan family cabins would be filled to the brim with visitors.

Dorcas set the standards high for Jane's wedding. She was unswerving in her resolve to have things done just her way for her only daughter's wedding.

"I'll have none of that riding for the kail," she lectured Jane as they were washing up the supper dishes on evening. "I never did like that ridiculous tradition."

"Yes, mother," sighed Jane. She'd heard the list of rules many times over the previous weeks and was growing weary of the lectures.

"And there'll be no shooting, either."

"Momma," Jane argued, "You know that Charles and his friends will be riding in, shooting off along the way and having a high old time. That's what all grooms do. You can't stop them from doing what they want when they are out on the road."

"I can't do anything about what they do along the way, but I won't have it once things get started here. You make sure those young men know that. And tell them they'd best not show up here in a sloppy, drunken state. There'll be enough drinking after the ceremony and that's acceptable as long as folks don't forget themselves. Besides, we don't want Charles getting drunk and then heaving it all back up during the ceremony." Jane crinkled her nose at the thought and then laughed.

"Momma, you worry too much. The groom and his men always visit and drink and shoot along the road on the way to the ceremony. You know that it's just what the young men do for every wedding."

"In my opinion, it's not a very appropriate practice. I expect Charles to keep to a more dignified manner on his wedding day."

"I don't know why. You never worry about such things any other day, why are you so worried about being so proper on my wedding day?"

"I beg your pardon. I am always proper. I might not be fancy or fussy, but I am always proper. And, young lady, folks will be watching what we Buchanans do on your wedding day. We will be as proper as any family around. Your father wouldn't have it any other way and I certainly won't either." Jane wisely decided to stop arguing with her mother for the lady of the manner had spoken and there would be no further debate about how things would proceed.

On the day of the ceremony, the bride walked down the stairs wearing a beige brocade gown that Dorcas had been sewing on for weeks. It wasn't the most practical gown for a young woman living along the river, as there weren't many balls or parties that she could ever wear it to later, but it was what Dorcas wanted. It was one of the few indulgences that Dorcas ever allowed in her life. Even her own wedding dress had been rather plain and sedate.

Isabella Mayne, a neighbor woman, had come to do Jane's hair up special before Dorcas and Isabella helped the blushing bride to get dressed. Dorcas lent Jane her mother's precious choker necklace, just for the day. It was her way of making sure her mother was included in this special day in some small way.

The sun was streaming in the front windows, making the tavern bright and cheery. The couple stood in front of the fireplace while Reverend Jessop, called in especially for the service, led them in reciting their brief vows. As soon as the vows were said, Henry, as the eldest male in the brides' family, began the party by offering the toast traditionally offered by the father of the bride.

The women hurried back to the kitchen and began bringing in heaping platters of ham and venison that the young men of the family had recently killed, along fresh fish and mussels from the stream that Dorcas had gathered herself. Large bowls were filled with potatoes and carrots. Baskets contained three different types of bread. The dessert table was laden with a large bride's cake flanked by bowls of sugared nuts and candies. The Buchanan men walked about with pitchers in hand, offering guests their choice of ale, cider and whiskey, keeping everyone's glasses full. The Buchanan women made sure that no one's plate went empty.

The drinking, dining, dancing and games continued from Friday afternoon until early Sunday morning when the Bibles came out and the worship service began. The hymns and the prayers were more sedate than usual, as many folks were struggling to recover from the excesses of two full days of revelry.

After the communal noon dinner, the wedding guests began to load their wagons to return to their homes. It was the biggest, most beautiful wedding that the valley had ever seen and Dorcas was filled with the pride and joy of a job well done. Dorcas had, as she vowed, done everything right and proper. Her Arthur would have been just as proud as she was.

Chapter Sixteen

It wasn't long after Buchanan-Magill wedding, that the trouble Thomas had forewarned his mother about did come along and disturb the peace of the valley. The native tribes once again began massive attacks on forts and small settlements all over the countryside. Frequent reports poured into the tavern as those fleeing the northern regions came through Old Town. Countless unfortunate settlers who hadn't had sufficient time to escape were killed or taken captive. Forts and homes alike were raided and burned to the ground. Even the British troops suffered casualties. Chaos reigned but it was a good distance from Old Town, at least for the time being.

The distance of the troubles helped the Buchanans stay calm and firmly rooted in their home. They soldiered on, trying to keep their everyday life as peaceable and productive as possible. They weren't about to turn and run again unless they absolutely had to.

In the early evening hours on a balmy evening in June, Dorcas was stirring chunks of ham into a large pot of beans cooking over the kitchen fire, while she waited for two pans of cornbread to come out of bake oven. The aroma of the beans and cornbread filled the entire house. Jane was bustling back and forth carrying dirty dishes into the kitchen and clean ones into the tavern.

Armstrong was in the front room, tending to customers and keeping it running as it should be. As he was wiping down the glasses that his sister brought in, he looked up to see a face that he'd never seen around these parts. That the man was unknown to him but that was not what worried him. He was used to seeing strange faces on a regular basis because the tavern sat at a heavily traversed crossroads.

What bothered him most about this stranger was the deeply troubled expression on the man's face. Like his father Arthur, Armstrong was adept at reading a person's thoughts just by looking at his brow and his eyes. What he had here was definitely a man seeking sanctuary and sustenance on his way to more protected locales. He had the look of man fleeing from imminent danger.

"Welcome, friend. What can I get for you?"

"A pint of ale and some grub, if you please," came the harried reply. He ran a grubby hand though his unruly hair.

"I'll pour you a pint and my sister will bring you some grub. Just sit wherever you please. Over by the fire is a favorite spot. Sit at the small table if you want to be alone or the long one if you want plenty of company." The man hung his hat on the back of a chair at the long table, sitting with his back to the fire. He propped his elbows on the table and was rubbing his forehead when Armstrong returned carrying his drink.

"Mind if I sit a spell with you," asked Armstrong.

"I'd welcome your company. Tell you the truth, it's been a couple of days since I've talked to anyone."

"I'm Armstrong Buchanan," he said, offering his hand.

"I'm Raymond Young," said the young man, taking Armstrong's hand.

"Raymond, if you don't mind my saying so, you look like something's troubling you deep down in your soul."

"There's plenty troubling me, and it ought to trouble anyone living around here. Some of the local Indians are on the warpath again. They already kilt a family over on the Youghiogheny and couple of men over near to Fort Pitt."

"What? That's the first I've heard tell of in a long time of any attacks in that area. What's stirring them up? I thought they'd signed a peace treaty."

"They did but then some of them went and broke the treaty. Seems they ain't happy with the way the soldiers are a treating them."

"Are they all revolting?"

"No, not all. Some Ottawa chief named Pontiac has been rallying his people and every other tribe that he can convince to join him. They've already gone after Fort Detroit, Fort Sandusky and Fort Michilimackinac. Word has it that he's aiming to take Fort Pitt, too. Guess those boys over near Fort Pitt were just a warm-up before they get to the fort itself."

"Hold on just a moment," suggested Armstrong. "My mother will want to hear this story."

Armstrong went to the kitchen to summon his mother and asked the traveler to repeat the disturbing news for her when she joined them. She listened carefully to every word the man said. She'd already made a firm decision before the man finished telling his tale.

"Sounds like we'd best pack up first thing in the morning and head back to Carlisle. If they're over to Pitt, we don't need to rush out tonight, but we don't want to chance staying here much longer." Even fiery Dorcas couldn't take on an entire league of warriors. "You are welcome to spend the night, Raymond, free of charge. Wouldn't be right to let a man sleep out in the open with everything going on as it is."

"I appreciate that, Mrs. Buchanan. I certainly do." He'd tried to sleep out in the open last night but was too afraid to close his eyes for very long, and exhaustion was threatening to overtake him. He'd sleep well tonight under the roof of this protective house.

"Ma, I think we'd best post some extra guards around the place, just in case. We haven't been keeping close watch lately but it sounds like we better do that till we can get out of here."

"I agree with you, Armstrong. You and your brothers take turns. I want at least two of you out there at all times, but I don't want you to get all tuckered out. I'll take a turn myself."

"But Ma . . ."

"Don't 'Ma' me, young man. You know that I've got the keenest eye and the best aim of all of you."

"There's certainly no arguing that."

"Your daddy liked to talk about the Buchanan motto, but did you ever hear my Armstrong clan motto?"

"Yes, Momma," he sighed. "I know you're very proud of it."

"I am proud of it, young man," she declared. "*I remain unvanquished.* When times get rough, I remember that phrase and what kind of stock I am made of. It revs me up to think on it. *I remain unvanquished.*"

When the Buchanans returned to Carlisle, they were shocked to find the town teeming with soldiers and other settlers seeking refuge from the recent uprisings. The narrow streets were full of pedestrians, horseback riders and carriages, all moving from shop to tavern to church to home. The Buchanans were aghast at the site and that they had to work their way slowly through the throngs to reach the tavern. When they reached the house on Main Street, they had to pull the wagons immediately to the back of the property to keep from blocking the road.

"Oh my goodness," cried out Sarah as she spied the wagons coming into the back yard. "Henry, Elizabeth, come quick! Dorcas and the others are all here!"

"What? They sent no word that they were coming," remarked a concerned Henry. "Are they all here? No one missing?"

Sarah did a quick headcount as the weary travelers dismounted the wagons.

"Yes! One and all are accounted for. And they appear to be good health."

Henry, Sarah and Elizabeth ran out to greet the returning family members. They were relieved and thrilled to see them.

"What happened to send you all packing," inquired Henry.

"Indians, of course," reported Robert.

"But what of the treaty," asked Elizabeth.

"Not all of the tribes are honoring the treaty. The rebel tribes are now worse than ever."

"Oh, I'm so sorry to hear that," moaned Sarah. "But I am glad to see that you all made it here unharmed and with your scalps still attached. Come in and eat. You must be starving after travelling all that way."

"And exhausted," added Elizabeth. "Sarah, you get them all fed, and I'll get the beds ready. I'm sure that they'll want to take to their beds fairly early this evening."

"Ah, you girls are wonderful," replied Dorcas. "We all could use a hearty meal and a good night's sleep. First, we need to get these wagons unloaded. If we wait until after we eat, I fear it won't get done tonight."

"We have plenty of hands and it won't take long," exclaimed Henry as he pulled the first trunk off the wagon. "Come now. We'll get this done in a snap."

Charles and William got the animals settled in the stable, while the rest of the men carried in everything that they'd been able to bring with them from the valley. Margaret followed Elizabeth upstairs to help pull bed covers from the cupboards and get the extra beds ready. Dorcas followed Sarah into the kitchen and immediately resumed control of her kitchen. In less than one hour, the family was neatly settled.

"Can't say that I'm glad to be back in the city but I sure am glad to see my family all around one table again," remarked Dorcas as they sat down to dinner that night. "It's been far too long since we've all been together."

"I know you prefer to be down by the creek, Momma, but we're glad that you're back here, out of danger," answered Henry.

"As good as it is to see your faces, I hope that we don't have to stay here too long. I can't believe how much Carlisle has grown and how busy it's come to be since we left. If this keeps up, it'll be a city as big as Philadelphia. You know I don't take too well to big city life."

"I understand your feelings completely, because I'd eventually like to get back there myself. Though, there is so much opportunity here right now, that it's a pretty good place to be, at least for the time being. A fella can make some good money if he's willing to roll up his sleeves and work for it. There's no reason why we can't all take advantage of some of those opportunities while we're here."

Henry's words proved to be right over the course of the following weeks and days. The tavern was busier than ever as more troops came to town and soldiers were sent to the Buchanan house for billeting. The tavern was filled wall-to-wall with activity all day, every day. Dorcas and her family spent every waking hour cooking, cleaning, changing bedding and pouring ale for dozens of refugees and soldiers. At mealtime, soldiers leaned against walls with their plates in hand because there weren't enough chairs to be had. At nighttime, every bed was crowded, oftentimes sleeping four or five persons in a bed meant for three.

Dorcas was thankful to have her entire brood with her to help control the chaos. As limitless as her energy might have appeared to be, she couldn't keep up with the demands that each day forced upon her without significant help. Still, nothing seemed to ruffle her feathers. Dorcas thrived in the midst of it. She was making money hand-over-fist now, money that would serve her family well for many years to come. That knowledge brought her great comfort. She didn't want for much herself but earning money for the benefit of her loved ones was one of her highest priorities.

The whole family enjoyed being once again in the heart of everything that was worth hearing. It was one small trade-off that made city life more tolerable for all of them. Between the soldiers, farmers, merchants and the lawmen who sat at their tables, there wasn't one bit of news or gossip that escaped their ears.

"I hear Bouquet is on his way here with nigh on 500 soldiers to defend Fort Pitt," claimed a baby-faced soldier, who was sitting in front of the fire playing checkers with another solider.

"Whew! 500 men? That sounds like an awful lot," answered his equally young companion.

"That's what he needs to fight these Indians. It's not just one tribe. The tribes have all banded together to create a big army of their own."

"Which tribes? Do you know?"

"Mingo and Lenape. Shawnee, too, I think."

"Ah, I've heard them Shawnee are mighty tough fighters."

"That's what I've heard, too. Sure I hope I don't have to face one of those fellows up close."

Come July, Colonel Henry Bouquet did indeed ride into Carlisle accompanied by his army of some 500 men. Some were English but many were Scots Highlanders, known to be fierce warriors in their homelands far across the sea. The Highlanders set up camp in pastures on the edge of town. Most of the Englishmen lodged in the homes and the businesses of locals, like the Buchanans. Truth be known, with her Scotch-Irish roots, Dorcas would have preferred to house the Scots rather than the Brits, but it was not her choice to make.

The large force had come to Carlisle to formulate and organize a battle plan before heading west to Fort Pitt. The fort had already survived several assaults by smaller contingents of Pontiac's forces but it was clear that a bigger attack was imminent. Several settlers and soldiers were held up in the fort but they didn't have enough men or ammunition to fend off a major attack without the help that Bouquet's troops would bring.

By early August, Bouquet's troops were ready to move forward and defend the fort. The English donned their red coats and the Scots their kilts. They marched off to the braying of the Scottish bagpipes.

As they marched down Forbes Road near Bushy Run, Bouquet's men were ambushed by an unusually large band of Indians. The troops fought valiantly, holding off the attackers until they eventually eased up as the sun went down. When the fighting stopped, the soldiers grabbed flour sacks from their food stores and constructed a redoubt on Edge Hill. They sheltered their injured soldiers and the horses in the redoubt for the night and braced themselves for another round of attacks.

While the soldiers worked on their fortification, Pontiac's forces increased their number and returned to Edge Hill, intending to launch another brutal battle at sunrise. The tribes had taken advantage of what they presumed to be a weak spot during the few minutes that the night sentries were being relieved by the morning ones.

Pontiac's men moved in as the nighttime guards walked away and the morning guards were just settling in, mistakenly thinking them unready to fight. However, the troops had been warned by scouts in the woods and were ready to fend off the attack. The night sentries merely pretended to walk away but instead they immediately turned back and ambushed the ambushers themselves. Pontiac's men fled in surprise and confusion. Bouquet's men then went on to Fort Pitt where they were able to defeat Pontiac's forces and save the fort.

Chapter Seventeen

As Pontiac's Rebellion raged on, Dorcas and her family stayed unscathed in Carlisle. They carried on their day-to-day life, just as they always had, impatiently awaiting the time when they could return to their beloved Kish Creek.

Dorcas was grateful for the security that Carlisle offered, but she dearly missed the beautiful blue-green valley and her home by the creek. She missed the refreshing breezes that blew through the valley. She was eager to get back home as soon as it was reasonably wise to do so. She watched the seasons come and go, always anxiously awaiting the first opportunity to load up the wagons and move one more time.

The late afternoon sun broke in and lit the serving room as Peter Adams strolled into the tavern. Dorcas was behind the bar, readying the tankards for the evening's customers.

"Peter, welcome! What a pleasure to see your face."

"Good day to you, Dorcas. You're looking well."

She came from behind the bar to greet him and offered him a seat.

"Please, sit down and make yourself comfortable."

"Oh no. I don't mean to sit and stay right now. I just came to ask you if it would be any trouble to have a little meeting here tonight."

"Tis no trouble at all but can I ask what the meeting is all about. Oh, never mind. I don't know why I even asked that. Just being nosey, I guess. It doesn't matter what it's about. You're always welcome here."

"I don't mind telling you about it at all, Dorcas. Besides, you'll be right here tonight and hearing every word of the meeting anyway. It's about that new Stamp Act. You've heard of it?"

"I have," she replied, not bothering to hide her disgust. "I don't right know what it is but it sounds like more taxes and I'm not anxious to share any more of my money with old King George."

"None of us are. We're all sick of paying these never-ending taxes. This one is all about paper goods."

"Paper goods? I don't understand."

"Parliament passed this ridiculous act demanding that all the paper goods that we buy or sell here in the colonies have an official tax stamp on them."

"Paper goods? You mean like writing paper?"

"Just about anything made of paper. What we've been told is any kind of legal documents, including wills, deeds and contracts have to have that darn stamp on them. All of our newspapers and magazines have to have them, too."

"Well, I never heard of such a thing!"

"Oh, and they even want playing cards to have the stamp."

"Well, I never! And how are we to come by these special tax stamps?"

"Word has it that they're sending over £100,000 worth of stamps and a bunch of the King's men to distribute them and collect the tax."

"Ha! They'll be hard-pressed to get that done, no matter how many stamps and how many men they send over."

"I forgot to mention that they aren't going to accept our paper money. They'll only take silver and gold coins to pay for it."

"That's preposterous! What is that Parliament doing to us? They keep putting these taxes on us but not giving us anything in return for our money."

"That's what tonight's meeting is all about. Some concerned local gents are going to put our heads together and see what we can do to stop this lunacy. We don't intend to pay it and we're going to let it be publicly known. We haven't organized ourselves yet, so I can't tell you how we're going to stop it, but stop it we will."

"I'll be happy to help you with that in any way that I can."

"They claim they need the money to pay their soldiers that they have here to protect us."

"That's hogwash. Those soldiers aren't doing anything these days. I haven't seen them do a lick of work since last winter. Matter of fact, I haven't seen them do much since that trouble over at Bushy Run. They sit around here, eating our food and drinking our ale and running up bills, leaving us stacks of paperwork to fill out to get paid for our troubles. They aren't doing anything worthwhile at all. Matter of fact, I think I run off those last two who were put up here with me. I kept giving them chores to do and wouldn't take no for answer. They left pretty quick after that started. I've got no patience for folks who don't work to earn their keep. Any grown, able body sleeping under my roof is going to earn it by paying or working. I'm thinking that the Parliament just wants us to finance their men's pensions."

"I think you're on to something there."

"I didn't pay any taxes under that Sugar Act they passed a couple of years ago and nobody ever paid any mind to that old Molasses Act either. Most folks around here are pretty smart about working around the Brit's rules. Most of us have started making our own wines and linens and such. We don't need to import things like we used to. We have our own ways nowadays."

"Well, I sure haven't talked to anybody here in town who intends to pay any more taxes to the Crown. Matter of fact, most of the local fellows have already decided that when those tax men come, they're going to make life rough enough to make them want to leave town on their own."

"Ha! It'll be mighty hard for old King George to collect his tax if he can't get his own men to do it."

"We plan to make our objections known and shut it down before it even starts."

"That's a good idea. How many will you be tonight?"

"I don't know for sure because word's getting around town right now. Maybe about 30 men."

"30? That's a fair number. I've got plenty of room for you, though, and you're all welcome to come."

"It's all settled then. We plan to meet just after sunset."

"I'll be ready for you."

The men held to their resolve and, after their meeting, they issued formal objections which were sent to England. Parliament predictably ignored their pleas. A few weeks later, the tax collectors came, bearing their stamps and ready for collection, despite the many, strong objections. They were not warmly met in the colonies. Most colonists ignored the tax and went about their daily business, leaving their paper goods unadorned by the abhorrent stamps.

Other locals were more assertive in their defiance of The Stamp Act. They made life miserable for the tax collectors, just as promised, harassing them on the streets and turning them out of local businesses. Eventually, the collectors gave up and went back home to England. The Stamp Act was officially repealed less than one year after it was enacted. Ironically, it wasn't worth the paper that it was written on.

When Pontiac's Rebellion died down completely and it appeared that it was safe to move, Dorcas decided to take her family back to Old Town, far away from soldiers lying around and all the other travails of city life. Her beloved valley would once again be home.

"Sure you don't want to stay in Carlisle, Dorcas," asked Harmon. "You've got a real nice business going here. You surely won't have near as many customers or make as much money over there as you do here."

"Oh, we've done better than you might think over there. Besides, this town living just isn't for me. I want to go back to the valley where I can breathe," she exclaimed with a wistful expression on her face. The wistful expression faded away and it was quickly replaced by a smirk. "And where folks don't look crossways at me just because I don't see fit to wear shoes when the weather's warm enough for it."

Harmon chuckled. There was something about his delightful cousin that never would be completely tamed. She'd dress up and go to church and be as graceful a lady as Carlisle had ever seen, but in her heart, she would always be a barefoot, salt-of-the earth, remarkably independent woman. There was no other woman on earth quite like her.

"Why don't you come with us this time, Harmon," she asked hopefully. She loved Harmon like a brother and wanted him to come live near them.

"Nah. I've got a fair business going on here and Carlisle agrees with me. Though I might ride over and visit you from time to time, if I'm welcome."

"You know that you'll always have a place at my table, Harmon, as well as a place to lay your head at night."

After the Buchanans returned to the valley, countless other settlers immediately followed their lead. It wasn't long before the tavern in the valley flourished once more.

Society was starting to bloom by the creek and *The Bounding Elk* was the home of that society. The circuit preacher and the circuit judge began visiting on a monthly basis, holding services and court by the hearth in the winter and in the shade of the trees in summer. In the winter of 1765, Dorcas hosted the biggest Christmas dinner and church service ever seen in the valley. Old Town was becoming an impressive settlement, in no small part due to the efforts of the Buchanan family.

Chapter Eighteen
1773

By 1773, William had died of the fever, leaving Margaret alone to raise their two small children. Armstrong was killed in a skirmish near Baltimore, never having married. He was buried somewhere around Baltimore but, as with many mothers of pioneer men, Dorcas would never learn exactly where he was laid to rest. The remainder of the Buchanan clan soldiered on, as they always had. Death and loss were simply a fact of life, something to born stoically. They had no choice but to bravely keep moving forward. They could not risk their own lives by over-indulging in long periods of mourning that might leave them vulnerable to attack.

Their grief was somehow made a little more bearable by the countless other things that they had to be grateful for. Death had failed to shrink the size of the family, thanks to recent and ongoing additions. Love and life had overcome the struggle for survival and the clan was now more than double the size of the original Buchanan family that had first moved to Kish Creek.

Arthur, Jr. had married the lovely Margery and set up housekeeping in Old Town, on property that adjoined his mother's land. Thomas and Elizabeth had filled their home with three sons and four daughters. William and Margaret had added two sons to the clan before he passed on. Jane had given birth to a son and a daughter. Robert, the youngest of Dorcas's children, was engaged to marry Lucinda Landrum in the coming year. The lands around the creek brimmed with Buchanans, making it the largest family for miles around. The locals often joked that, because there were so many of them, that the town should probably be called Buchanan Town rather than Old Town.

In May of '73, the Crown lobbed another insult at the settlers in the form of the Tea Act. This particular act piled more taxes on top of the taxes already in effect under the Townsend Acts. The colonists were once again outraged.

The men talked about openly rebelling against the new act while the women rebelled by making their own untaxable tea. Dorcas, like many pioneer women, grew lavender and other herbs in her garden to make her own special blend to enjoy and she, as any of the women did, traded or sold her tea to neighbors and friends. The colonists had had their fill of abuse from the Crown and would no longer tolerate whatever burdens King

George decided to send their way. By December, the resistance was nearing the breaking point.

"Did you hear what happened in Boston," Horace asked Arthur while they sat in front of the fire one evening, playing checkers and catching each other up on all the news that they'd heard.

"I hear tell of lots of things happening in Boston. Pray tell, what story do you have to share?"

"Some folks fed up with the tea tax took matters in their own hands."

"Did they start an uprising?"

"In a manner of speaking," Horace chuckled.

"In a manner of speaking? Don't toy with me. Tell me the whole story."

"A bunch of fellas boarded a couple of tea ships that were anchored in the harbor. They dressed up like Indians, painted their faces and all, so they wouldn't be recognized. Then they went all wild, busting things up and throwing every bit of the tea in the cargo holds right into the bay. They're calling it *The Boston Tea Party.*" Arthur laughed out loud at the pictures forming in his mind.

"That'll show 'em," Dorcas claimed as she came to the table with a pitcher of ale to refill their tankards.

"The Brits are mad as hell. They want the folks that did it punished, of course."

"Where are folks saying it'll all lead, all this standing up against the King," asked Arthur.

"War, eventually. Where else could it lead? You know he's never going to stop trying to make a profit off of us. None of us want to be taxed without having a voice in Parliament and the Brits are never going to let any colonists have a voice. Folks are saying it's all building up to a full-on war twixt us and the Brits."

"Well, it's been an awful long time coming but coming it is. It appears as though that day is fast approaching," answered Arthur. "I just hope we're ready to truly fight for what's right."

Chapter Nineteen
1774

May arrived and brought with it fierce thunderstorms that ravaged the valley for three days, leaving streams of muddy water running down every slope, large or small. On the third day of storms, the afternoon had been so dark that it was hard to tell when afternoon ended, and the evening hours began. The wide dirt roads that intersected at *The Bounding Elk* were no longer traversable because the mud was deep enough to swallow wagon wheels, horse hooves and boots all alike. Those few folks who braved the weather were forced to create their own paths wherever patches of higher, dryer ground allowed.

No travelers were lodging with the Buchanans at the time, so the tavern was empty and quiet all afternoon. No townsfolk saw fit to brave the weather or the road conditions merely for the sake of the tavern's society. Only Dorcas and Robert were in the main house because the rest of the family had been holed up in their own cabins since the storms started. The only breaks in the stillness came when thunder rolled across the valley and shook the whole place, rattling the doors, windows and dishes.

Right in the midst of a particularly violent round of wind, rain and thunder, the door flew open, blowing two strangers into the comfortable warmth of the tavern. They looked as though they had just emerged from the seas rather than from the road, with water drizzling down from the brims of their hats onto their thick, blond beards, before trickling down their long coats onto the floor.

The strapping, handsome young men, about eighteen and twenty years of age, were smiling and laughing despite the treacherous weather. They stood in front of the door, shaking off as much water as they could before walking further into the room.

"Welcome, gentlemen. Have yourselves a seat and hang your coats next to the fire to dry out," suggested Dorcas, nodding to a table in front of the hearth. "What'll you have this evening?"

"Whatever you got to eat," exclaimed the bigger of the two boys. "We're powerful hungry."

"And whatever you got to drink," exclaimed the younger, chuckling. "We're powerful parched, too. I swear to you that anything you have on hand will do."

"Well, I got some venison stew and a loaf of hardy bread to eat. I've got whatever you want to drink, including whiskey, cider and ale. If you don't mind a suggestion, the whiskey would be best to warm you up well enough," she offered.

"That'll do just fine, ma'am, if you please."

"We was wondering, ma'am, do you have beds available this evening? That storm promises to stay a while and we're not particularly fond of the idea of being out in it."

"I sure do and you're welcome to 'em. You just get warm and dry now, and then we'll get you settled in later. I'll bring your whiskey first and get your grub in just a minute. I'm Dorcas, by the way."

"Appreciate it, ma'am. I'm Samuel and this is my younger brother, Stephen."

"Pleased to meet you. I'll be right back with your whiskey." She turned to go to the bar but stopped in her tracks and turned back to her two guests.

"What did you do with your horses?"

"They're tied up under that big tree beside the house for now," answered Samuel.

"That won't do. You can't leave those poor creatures out in this tempest. There's a barn out behind the house where you can bed them down and give them some hay. Let 'em sleep out of the rain tonight."

"Thank you much, ma'am," answered Samuel.

"There's no sense us both going out there again. I'll go take care of them both," offered Stephen. He downed his whiskey, grabbed his hat and coat and went back out into the storm.

Just as Stephen was stepping back in and shaking the rain off for a second time, Dorcas returned, bearing big bowls of steaming venison stew, a platter of thick bread and a bowl of creamy butter.

"Ah, that food smells might tasty. Could you please bring us another round of that whiskey? It's certainly helping to take the chill off," said Samuel.

"I'll be happy to." She grabbed the glasses from the table and returned with them filled to the top.

"Tell me, Samuel, what brings you and your brother to these parts in this dreadful weather?"

"We're looking for a place to settle down. Coming from New York. Been living there with our folks but we want to find some land to settle on somewhere around these parts. We're not really all that partial to New York."

"We'd definitely be proud to have you as neighbors, young man," she said with a warm smile. "How long you been traveling?"

"We've exploring these hills and valleys for a few weeks now."

"Have you met any folks in your travels? Do you hear any news that you can share?"

"A little here and there. Everyone's mostly talking about the massacre of the Mingos over at Yellow Creek." Dorcas gasped at the pronouncement.

"Yellow Creek? Not Chief Logan's village?"

"Aye, Logan was the name we heard tell of," answered Stephen as he returned to the table.

Her heart sank at the thought of harm coming to her old friend Logan.

"He's a good friend of my family. Was he wounded?"

"From what we heard, he wasn't there. His family was all killed, though. Brutally slaughtered, actually." Samuel didn't find it necessary, or even possible, to sugarcoat the details.

"No!" Dorcas was horrified. Tears filled her eyes. "Tell me what happened." Samuel began to tell the story while Stephen wolfed down his dinner and Dorcas sat at his side, listening numbly.

"The story going around is that two brothers by the name of Greathouse heard that the chief was out on a hunt with most of the men of his tribe, so they decided to attack the village while they were away."

"They attacked innocent women and children?"

"They sure did."

"Oh no," she wailed. "What scoundrels! Did they attack in the night while they were sleeping? I know Logan's wife and she's a fighter. She'd put up a good fight if she could. She'd do anything and everything possible to protect her family."

"They went after them in broad daylight. They walked right into their camp, acting like friends."

"Those evil snakes," she snarled.

"Snakes is right. A couple of Logan's men had stayed behind to protect their family, so Greathouse took them some rum and was acting like they were great friends. He asked them over to Joshua Baker's cabin up the river a piece. They got them drunk and then challenged them to do some target shooting. Once the Mingo's' guns were empty, the Greathouse men turned and started shooting all the Indians. After the men were dead, they went back started on the women and children. They killed Logan's wife, brother, pregnant sister and a bunch of others. Cut them up after they shot them, too. Even the baby that his sister was carrying. Cut him right out of his mother and scalped him."

"Dear Lord in Heaven," she cried. "A baby not even born yet? Are these men or devils?"

"Devils, for sure."

"Poor Logan. He must be overcome by shock and grief. He saved our whole family more than once by warning us that trouble was coming. I wish that I could do something for him now but there's nothing in this world that I could do that would ease his terrible pain. My heart aches for him and his family."

"He might be grieving but it brought out the warrior in him. He's fighting back and he's vowed revenge. Said he's going to kill ten white men for every one of his kin that were killed. He's rounding up every warrior that he can find and going out on the warpath."

"Oh no, no, no," Dorcas cried. "Such a terrible, terrible thing." She sat still, looking into the fire, softly sighing and moaning. She was sick with grief for Logan. "But who could blame the poor man? How could any soul endure be expected to endure such blow?"

"Don't rightly know, ma'am," answered Stephen.

"He's always been such a good friend to the white men. Why, he used to come visit often and sit at this very table, talking to everyone in the place. He was as good a man as I ever met. He was so kind and so extraordinarily intelligent. I always enjoyed his visits. He always had something to say that was worth listening to."

"Someone told me that his name was John Logan and that his daddy was a white man. Is that true?"

"We never called him anything but Logan, so I can't answer to his name for sure. Might have been John. Might have been James. But now his daddy, I do know about that. He told me that his father was Chief Shikellamy, an Oneida. I believe I once heard him tell another fella that his mother was a Cayuga. I'll tell you though, all I really know for sure is that he was a good and decent man down to his bones."

The entire story having been told and the horror of it all revealed, the three sat and stared at the fire without talking. The inhumanity of the attacks was too tragic and too sickening for anyone to fully comprehend.

"And those Greathouse boys, what of them," Dorcas asked once she recovered her senses. "Will they be made to pay the price for their terrible crimes? Surely they will be brought to justice for what they've done."

"I don't know. At first, some thought Michael Cresap was responsible. The story about it being the Greathouse brothers just came out in recent days. Folks say Logan still believes it was Cresap."

"Michael Cresap? Is he kin to that awful Thomas Cresap that caused all that trouble about thirty years ago?"

"I heard tell that Thomas Cresap was Michael's father."

"So, wickedness just runs in their blood, eh? What a disgraceful family they must be. More like a pack of wild wolves than a family." Dorcas was incensed and saddened by the senseless killings. She knew those people who were killed. She respected and cared about those people. They had been her neighbors. More than that, they had been her friends.

Lord Dunmore, the governor of Virginia, after hearing that Logan had put the Shawnee and Mingo tribes on the warpath, declared war on the native tribes. Any sensible man would have done all that he could to reach out to Logan and work for peace, but Dunmore chose war instead. Leave it to the Brits to choose force over reason. The war raged on for most of the year after the attacks.

Many tribes wanted to negotiate a peace settlement but Logan persisted. He had the hunger and, in some folks' opinions, he had every right to retaliate the loss of his family. He was proving to be relentless in his quest.

It wasn't until the British won the Battle of Point Pleasure in October of that year that a treaty was finally signed and peace was restored. Most of the tribes joined in the treaty but Logan would understandably have no part of the negotiations. Instead, he sent Lord Dunmore a letter that touched the hearts of many and was eventually printed in newspapers across the colonies.

> *Logan's Lament*
>
> *I appeal to any white man to say, if ever he entered Logan's cabin hungry, and he gave him not meat; if ever he came cold and naked, and he clothed him not. During the course of the last long and bloody war, Logan remained idle in his cabin, an advocate for peace. Such was my love for the whites, that my countrymen pointed as they passed, and said, Logan is the friend of white men. I had even*

thought to have lived with you, but for the injuries of one man. Col. Cresap, the last spring, in cold blood, and unprovoked, murdered all the relations of Logan, not sparing even my women and children. There runs not a drop of my blood in the veins of any living creature. This called on me for revenge. I have sought it: I have killed many: I have fully glutted my vengeance. For my country, I rejoice at the beams of peace. But do not harbour a thought that mine is the joy of fear. Logan never felt fear. He will not turn on his heel to save his life. Who is there to mourn for Logan? Not one.

Logan continued his vengeful campaign until his death.

Chapter Twenty
1775

Life in the valley went on relatively peacefully for a few months but every resident harbored the knowledge that a full-on war, the likes of which they'd not yet seen, was lurking just around the corner. They nervously awaited the devastation they were certain was coming. The patriots were fed up with unjust British rule and the seemingly endless demands for more and more taxes without any representation in Parliament, protection from enemy forces or the even most basic rights of British citizenship. The abuses simply would not be tolerated much longer.

In May of 1775, newspapers and correspondence arrived from points east, reporting on several battles being fought in Massachusetts. The first letters that came were from relatives who still lived near Philadelphia and Boston. Their missives were a frightening mix of fact, rumors and supposition. The newspapers were only slightly more enlightening. The colonists had had enough of the British, and the Massachusetts militia had opened fire on the Regulars in Lexington and Concord. The long simmering tensions had finally reached a breaking point and a full-on war for independence was raging.

Later that month, the official word came that a bigger militia was needed to assist the Continental Army and a call to arms was issued. Old Town became a major rallying point for the men of the militia, with hundreds of men coming from all over the valley to serve. Whether they were farmers, weavers, masons or millers, they instantly became soldiers. Each man packed up his haversack, guns and ammunition, then marched off to fight for his freedom and that of others.

Kish Valley became the militia headquarters, largely because of Arthur. Before the war broke out, he'd been laying out and selling nearby lots for a town he intended to call Derry. That all ended when the war began. He had a reputation as a skilled fighter and a natural-born leader, so it wasn't long before farmer and developer Arthur Buchanan, Jr. became Captain Arthur Buchanan.

Armstrong's one-room log cabin had remained empty after his death, so it became the center of operations for Arthur and other leaders of the local company. The main house, the outlying family cabins and the outbuildings, along with the considerable land that the Buchanans had acquired over the past few years, including Arthur's planned town of Derry, allowed plenty of space for the troops to gather. Old Town became a large, thriving military camp with long rows of white tents filling the empty spaces between the tavern and the other cabins.

While the men organized, planned their strategies and practiced target shooting, the Buchanan women worked from sunup to sundown, and often even later when the moonlight and candlelight would assist their efforts. It seemed that the men grew more restless and agitated at night, something that Dorcas rightfully attributed to the ale. She noticed that they were much more anxious to march unto battle late at night after a couple of stiff drinks than they were over breakfast in the clear light of day.

Arthur had insisted that his brother's move themselves and their families into the upstairs bedrooms of the tavern for their own comfort and safety during these tumultuous times. The women all readily agreed that it would be better if they stayed together under one roof so that they could better help with the seemingly endless needs of the children, the tavern and the camp. Dorcas was mindful and appreciative of the fact that each of her sons had married women whose strength and independence almost rivaled her own. There was no room in this situation for women who thought themselves to be delicate flowers or above good, hard work.

That small band of Buchanan women worked just as hard for the cause as the men in the camp did. While the tavern had become the meal hall for the militia, it also still functioned as a tavern for locals and occasional strangers passing through. The ladies cooked and served food and drink for everyone living within five miles of the tavern. They toiled over the laundry and the mending for the family, as well as the troops. They tended to the children, the garden, the livestock and the fires with unfailing diligence. Arthur might be leading an army of men, but his mother was just as busy leading her own small troop of women caring for his men.

When supplies predictably began to run low, Arthur started sending regular supply wagons back to Carlisle for the food and other supplies that couldn't be replenished by hunting and foraging parties. The forest provided plenty of venison, turkeys, rabbits and squirrels to put on the table, as well as nuts and berries. However, the Buchanan hens could not keep up with egg production, nor could the cows keep up with the demands for milk. Flour ran out quickly, as did tea and coffee. Arthur dispatched supply wagons to Carlisle every two weeks to fulfill the increased needs of his family and the camp.

The protective mountains tended to keep the war away from Old Town and every other settlement in Kish Valley. However, while the war waged on far to the east, the British had encouraged the Indians to attack settlements from the west and to keep moving east while the Regulars moved west. Arthur was faced with the difficult decision of how many men to march into battle and how many to leave encamped, ready and able to defend Old Town. He could not, in good conscience, leave the settlements in the valley vulnerable, yet he'd received word that his troops were sorely needed in eastern Pennsylvania and New Jersey. He was also aware that some of his men would prefer to stay behind to defend their families and their homes.

After many long consultations with his most trusted advisors, Arthur decided to split his troops in two. Half of them would stay to protect the valley, while the other half would go east to join the Continentals.

Chapter Twenty-One
1776

Near the end of March, a courier brought orders to Arthur to send his men to Carlisle. They were being summoned to New York, along with troops from all over Pennsylvania. Thousands of men trudged through the melting snow and mud, arriving in New York in late April, only to be ordered on to Albany, where they joined a larger force preparing to attack Quebec. It would be the middle of June by the time they arrived in that great northern city.

Arthur sent letters home whenever he could, which wasn't often. It wasn't until after the battle at Quebec that he could write.

> *Quebec, June 15, 1776*
> *My Dearest Mother,*
> *Worn to the bone. Some are fighting barefoot. We lost over 60 men. Some were killed and some are missing, presumed captured. My men, and indeed all of the others, have all been giving it all they have. However, we had to retreat as our losses were too*

great. We didn't lose any of my men from home in the battle but, after the retreat, some of them, thinking they were out of danger, took off from camp without weapons and were immediately attacked by Indians who had been watching them. It is with great sadness that I must tell you that they kilt Abdiel McAllister. He was the only one of my men to be lost.
I do not know when we will return to Old Town but I do hope that it will be soon. All of my men are in desperate need of good food and a good rest.
With all my love,
Arthur

Dorcas laid the letter on the table after having read it aloud to the womenfolk while they took a break from their afternoon chores to enjoy their lunch.

"It might be selfish to say so, but I am awfully glad that Arthur is alive and not wounded."

"I don't care if it is selfish to say so. I'm thankful to God and very much relieved," noted Arthur's young wife.

"Our thoughts might be selfish, but our actions certainly won't be. We'll go over and pay a call on Abdiel's widow and parents, and offer them what help we can whilst they are in mourning."

"Momma, do you think that a wise thing to do? What if we're attacked on the road," asked Jane.

"I will not let that family mourn alone. It's just half a morning's ride from here. We'll gather up half-a-dozen of the men from camp to go with us. I honestly doubt we'll see any trouble t'wixt here and there but we'll take the men just the same. There's no sense in taking senseless chances. Margery, as Arthur's wife, you really must come along with me. After all, Abdiel was one of his men."

"I wouldn't have it any other way," replied Margery. "I was just sitting here thinking on what we ought to take over to them."

"Jane, you stay here and keep things going right. It'll be quiet here during hours that we're away."

"Yes, ma'am." Jane was glad to be relieved of the calling duty. She didn't much like leaving the house these days and she was wise to question the wisdom of paying a social call, no matter how great the need for comfort might be.

As regular reports poured in from the west about attacks both to the east and the west of Kish Valley, tension permeated the air. No soul rested easy in the dark of night or even in the bright light of the day. No woman dared so much as hang out laundry in her own yard without at least one-armed protector watching over her. No man dared venture out to hunt without two or three others riding along. This mission of mercy could turn out to be an utterly dangerous undertaking, but Dorcas would not be deterred.

"Let's get to doing some baking tonight and then we'll pack it up and head that way as soon the sun comes up tomorrow. You girls get back in the kitchen and start cooking. I'll go round up the best men I can find and give them their orders."

"Dorcas, sometimes I wonder if they should have sent you to lead the troops instead of Arthur. I believe you'd give orders to George Washington himself."

"I'd give them to King George, if the crazy old fool would listen to reason just once."

"Not a one of us doubts that," chuckled Jane.

Margery and Dorcas were up before the sun, loading baskets of food into the wagon to be delivered to the grieving McAllister family. Eight of the men in the camp volunteered to accompany the women on their journey. They wanted to pay their respects to the family of their fallen comrade just as much as they wanted to protect the two Buchanan women. The women were quite well-protected with two men riding along on each side of their wagon.

As they neared the McAllister cabin, they were surprised to see the house wide open and the McAllisters outdoors tending to their regular chores as if everything was normal. There wasn't a bit of black bunting anywhere on the house and none of the family was clad in black. Something wasn't right.

"What do you make of that," asked Margery, as they drew near to the cabin.

"I don't know what to think. They certainly don't look as though they're in mourning," answered Dorcas.

"You don't suppose they haven't been told yet, do you?"

"Surely they were told before we were."

"What do we do now? We don't want to be the ones to have to tell them."

"Let's go on up and give them the food, and tell them that we were thinking of them, then see if they say anything about him after that."

"I'd appreciate it if you'd do all the talking, Dorcas. I'm afraid that I'll slip up and make a mess of things."

"Don't you worry. I'll get this sorted out."

Mrs. McAllister spied the wagon and escorts approaching and she greeted them with a hearty smile and an enthusiastic wave.

"Mrs. Buchanan! What an unexpected pleasure to see you! What brings you all the way over here?"

"I was just thinking about you, Mrs. McAllister, and it troubled me how long it's been since we've seen each other. How are you doing?" She stood on the porch, basket in hand, eagerly anticipating a reply that would guide her in the right direction.

"I couldn't be better! We just got the happiest news about Abdiel."

"Oh really? Do tell. I always appreciate hearing good news."

"Well, it didn't start out happy. It started out terrible. We first got news that he'd been wounded and was missing, presumed dead. Then just two days ago, we got word that he's alive and that he's been released in a prisoner exchange."

"That's wonderful news!"

"We were in grieving for a few days, and it was as terrible as anything I've ever gone through. But when we found out that he was alive, the whole mess felt like nothing more than a bad dream. He's coming home soon to rest up and heal from his wounds. They say he'll recover completely if he rests up and takes care of himself."

"Oh, Abigail, that's quite a turn of events," exclaimed Dorcas as Margery sighed with relief. "I am so happy for you all."

"You ladies come in now and let's visit a bit. What do you have in that basket there?"

"Some baked goods for your family, pies and such."

"Sounds wonderful. Let's spread it out on the table and have ourselves a right fine little celebration."

"We'd be honored to. It isn't often that we get happy news from the battlegrounds."

Just a few weeks later, late on a steamy afternoon, another post rider came into the tavern and dropped a heavy satchel onto the bar. Dorcas was bustling about, taking care of the early supper crowd but she paused long enough to see what the rider had brought to her door. She always looked forward to seeing whatever came in the post.

"Good afternoon to you, Abner. Do you have any good news to share to this evening?"

"I'll say, Mrs. Buchanan," he answered as he opened his bag and dug into its depths. "Got a bunch of letters and packages in my bag for you but nothing compares to what's in this here newspaper," he quipped as he pulled out a small stack of newspapers and handed one to Dorcas. "Wait till you lay your eyes on *The Pennsylvania Evening Post*."

"Something exciting in there?"

"Just about the most exciting to ever have happened."

"Well, let me see that for myself," she said as she took the paper from his hand. "You take a seat and my girls will fetch you something to eat. It's on the house today." Dorcas took the paper outside, so she could sit down on the bench by the front door and read the paper by the last light of the day. It was soon apparent that what Abner had said, that it was the most exciting to ever have happened, was quite true.

> *The Pennsylvania Evening Post, Saturday July 6, 1776. In CONGRESS, July 4, 1776. A Declaration by the representatives*

of the United State of America, in General Congress assembled.

When in the course of human events, it becomes necessary for one people to dissolve the political bands which have connected them with another, and to assume among the powers of the earth, the separate and equal station to which the Laws of Nature and of Nature's God entitle them, a decent respect to the opinions of mankind requires that they should declare the causes which impel them to the separation.

We hold these truths to be self-evident, that all men are created equal, that they are endowed by their Creator with certain inalienable rights, that among these are life, liberty and the pursuit of happiness.

Dorcas spent the next hour reading, stopping occasionally to stare out at the creek and mull over what she'd read before turning back to read some more, until she reached the end of the story. Once she'd read it to the end twice, she sat a while longer, watching the sun approach the western horizon and thinking about the marvel she had just read and what the ramifications might be now and in the years to come.

Once her heart and mind had settled and her thoughts were straight, Dorcas walked back into the tavern.

"Jane, hand me one of those tacks."

Jane reached behind the counter and pulled out a small box of tacks. "What are you doing, Momma?"

"Hanging this up for all to see," she explained as she posted the newspaper to the inside of the door. "Abner, you got any more copies of that newspaper you can spare for me?"

"Of course, I do. You know I always bring a few. I brought extra this time because I knew lots of folks would want to see this for themselves."

"Can you give me two more?"

"Sure can." He handed them over and Dorcas posted one by the bar and one on the fireplace mantel.

"I do want as many folks as possible to see this. I want them to read every word of it. Oh, how I wish that my dear Arthur was here to see this day. He would be so pleased. So very pleased, indeed." Dorcas couldn't help but think that perhaps that the unimaginable risks the settlers took every day of their lives would all be worth it. Perhaps all of this strife might eventually come to a good end.

Chapter Twenty-Two
1777

In January, Arthur was ordered to round up 50 of his men from home to go on a scouting tour near Princeton, New Jersey. The smaller the troop he was commanded to take, the more selective he was of who he picked. He meant to select from among the sharpest minds and the sharpest shots that could be found under his command. Still, Arthur was mindful not to rely on the same men over and over. He didn't want to drive them to exhaustion. He rotated his best men in and out on each tour. For Princeton, he selected Lieutenants James McClure and William Wilson to ride along with him, allowing each of them to handpick soldiers from their own units but giving them the same cautious advice about not wearing out their best men too severely. Once the company arrived on the east coast, they joined the Continental Army in several battles, staying on until they were sent home just before the onset of summer.

They made the long ride back to Kishacoquillas Valley and awaited their next call to arms. Come July, Arthur organized a full battalion, the official Fifth Battalion of Cumberland County, with the intent of protecting

Mifflin County. Their mere presence provided extra protection to those living in and around Old Town. When marauding native tribes approached looking for victims, they could clearly see that they were outnumbered by the Arthur's battalion, so they moved on to easier targets outside valley and out of the view of the troops.

More orders came in August, directing Arthur to lead his men to Long Island. Their orders were to go east as soon as possible. Arthur sent several riders out into the valley to summon his men to duty once more. Every able-bodied man, regardless of age, was being called either to battle or to protect Old Town. Be they 14 or 40, if they could shoot a gun, they were recruited.

On the morning before their departure, heat and humidity hung heavy in the air. Windows were open on both sides of the tavern in an attempt to cool the rooms. Dutch doors at the front and back of the tavern usually were only open on the top, but on this day, they were propped wide open in the vain hope of allowing cooler air to flow through. Unfortunately, not even the slightest breeze wafted in from any direction.

The Buchanan ladies were fighting the sweltering heat and serving a room packed with hungry, sweaty, anxious men. The men rolled their sleeves up, wiped their brows with their kerchiefs and guzzled ale in futile attempts to cool themselves. The Buchanan women pinned their damp curls up off their necks, fanned themselves and guzzled lemonade when their hands weren't full of serving dishes.

Meanwhile, Arthur assembled his officers in Armstrong's cabin, now his makeshift headquarters, to plan their departure and prepare their men to join the Continentals. Orders went out for one and all to be ready to move come the break of dawn. Every man in the camp was busy preparing for the long march and the battles that lay ahead.

Several of the men had gone up the hill several yards away from the tents and cabins, to a clearing where they spent several hours shooting mark to sharpen their skills. The shots rang out again and again and echoed across the valley throughout the better part of the afternoon.

In a moment that would live on in Dorcas's memory for the rest of her life, the shots suddenly stopped. One split-second later, frantic yelling filled the banks of the creek. The small hairs on the back of Dorcas's neck stood up and her body began to shake uncontrollably. The target practice area was only half a mile from the house, well within hearing distance of the tavern.

Dorcas could tell from the commotion that something had gone horribly wrong. Someone surely must be gravely injured. She dropped the pitcher of ale that she'd been carrying onto the nearest table and ran as fast as her legs would carry her towards the uproar, her heart filling with dread at what she might find there. It felt to her that time stood still as she flew up that hill.

She pushed her way through a circle of men to see what was going on and what she saw caused her knees to go weak, her head to spin and her stomach to churn. It was a mother's worst nightmare realized.

Lucinda, Robert's wife, had followed Dorcas out of the house, burst onto the scene and screamed out in horror at what she saw. Thomas was laying on his back beneath a large oak tree. Blood oozed from a large hole in the center of his forehead. His three oldest sons stood nearby, dumbfounded. His brothers were desperately working to save him, but Dorcas could see that it was too late. There was nothing that could be done to stop the bleeding and save him. The bullet had done performed its tragic, fateful work in an instant.

"Boys, stop," she called out softly. "He's already gone." His brothers cried out in anguish, as their mother knelt to her son and, just as she had done with Arthur several years prior, gently closed his eyes for the final time.

"Let's get him to his place now," she said, barely able to choke out the words. A soldier standing beside her offered his hand and helped Dorcas to her feet. It took every bit of resolve she could muster to stay upright and in her right mind. She felt as though she wasn't really present, as if this was all really a nightmare from which she would awake at any minute. She kept moving and she kept talking but nothing felt real to her.

"Henry, you go fetch Elizabeth from the tavern and bring her back to their place."

Henry nodded, turned around and set off the most dreaded errand of his life. Not only was he trying to work through his own shock and horror, but now he would have to tell Elizabeth that her beloved husband had just been killed. As he walked down the hill, he struggled to think of the right words to say to the new widow. He'd seen men shot and killed before but, up until now, it had never been one of his brothers. Like his mother, Henry felt like none of this could possibly be real. When Dorcas had run out of the tavern, all of her customers had followed her. Every resident of Old Town knew the sound of tragedy in the air – chaos and panic, followed by an eerie silence. Every person visiting the tavern and everyone who lived within earshot, ran out see what horrible tragedy had befallen the community this afternoon. Initially, Jane and Elizabeth had stayed behind to keep things in order but Elizabeth was now making her way to the scene.

Henry met her halfway back to the tavern. He took her by the shoulders and looked her directly in the eyes. He needn't say one word. She could tell by the look in his eye that her husband was gone. Overwhelmed, she gasped for air three times before collapsing into her brother-in-law's arms. He lifted her up and carried her back to the tavern. He wanted to make sure that Thomas was back in their cabin and cleaned up, and that she had ample time to absorb the devastating news, before he took her back to her home and her late husband.

Jane was alone in the tavern when Henry burst in, carrying in their sister-in-law. He laid her on the long bench just inside the door.

"Elizabeth!" Jane cried out in shock. "Henry, what happened to her?"

"Bless her, she just couldn't take the news." Jane ran to get a damp cloth to cool Elizabeth's brow and bring her around.

"What news? What's happened?"

"It's Thomas."

"No, no, no. God, no. Please don't tell me," She wailed. Like Elizabeth, she didn't need to hear that her brother was dead. Her eldest brother's face told the story. She suddenly felt herself falling into that nauseating, surreal state that the rest of her family had already come to.

"He's been shot dead." Jane moaned in agony as Henry continued. "It was an accident. He was setting the targets for Robert and the gun had a hang-shot. Thomas stepped out from behind the tree to see what was taking so long and, just as he did, the shot finally fired."

"No. Oh no. Robert was shooting?"

"Yes. I'm afraid so." The reality was beginning to settle in, and Henry's stoic demeanor began to crumble. He turned his face away from the women in a futile attempt to hide his emotions. Jane struggled to restrain her own sobs while she tended to Elizabeth, but she wept for both her brothers, as well as Elizabeth and her mother. This one horrible accident had born so many victims.

Elizabeth began to come around and as she did, she wept and moaned, building from a soft cry to an eventual uncontrollable sobbing. When she'd cried all that she could cry for the time being, she sat up and looked at Henry.

"Where is he? Where is my Thomas," she asked softly.

"They're taking him to your place right now."

"I must go to him. I have to go."

"We'll walk you there," he said as he helped Elizabeth sit up. "Jane, shut the place up for now. Everyone will be over Tom's house, at least till dark anyway. And no one's going to want to eat for a while. No one will have the stomach for it."

The three of them walked side by side, Henry supporting Elizabeth on her left side and Jane on her right. By the time they reached the Holt cabin, it was surrounded by dozens of solemn soldiers. The crowd parted as the bereaved trio approached. Dorcas met them at the door and replaced Jane at Elizabeth's side.

They walked her to where Thomas had been laid on the bed in the corner. She sat beside him and collapsed onto his chest, clinging to him and wailing. Her children gathered round her, uneasy and unsure of how to help their mother, or each other, in these tragic moments.

Nearly half an hour later, she sat up and turned to face Henry once again.

"Tell me what happened," she sniffled and Henry recalled the sorrowful tale.

"Where is Robert now," she asked.

"He is still up at that tree. He is overcome with guilt and grief. They can't get him to come back down to the house."

"I must go see him."

"Now Elizabeth, you know Robert didn't aim to hurt Thomas. You know how close they were. His heart is breaking. It wasn't his fault. It truly wasn't," counseled Henry.

"I know that. That's why I want to go to him. He should be told that he's not to blame." Elizabeth had the same gracious and understanding manner as her mother-in-law.

"I'll go with you, dear," said Dorcas. "Maybe those men can't get him to leave that infernal tree but I'm sure that you and I can. We'll pick him up and carry him away, if we have to."

The two women walked up to the site and found Robert sitting beneath the tree, staring at puddle of his brother's blood. He appeared to be in a trance, oblivious to everything going on around him. Lucinda was on her knees beside him, rubbing his back and whispering into his ear.

"Robert, come along now. It's time go home," said Dorcas.

"Listen to your mother, Robert. You need to do as she says," encouraged Lucinda. He neither moved nor spoke. Elizabeth kneeled down on the ground in front of her brother-in-law.

"Robert," whispered Elizabeth. "Robert." Still he did not move. She put her hand on his cheek and turned his gaze away from the blood to her. Avoiding looking at the blood herself, she looked deep into Robert's eyes.

"Darling Robert, this is not your fault. It was an accident." His red eyes filled with tears again as her touch broke his trance and he finally spoke.

"But I pulled the trigger."

"Yes, but he stepped out from behind the tree. It was not your fault. It wasn't his fault either. It was just a terrible, terrible accident."

"How can I ever live with myself again?"

"You have to. You have to accept that it was an accident and pull yourself together for your mother and for Lucinda. And for me. I'm going to need your help now more than ever, dear brother. We're all going to need you more now." She would have said anything to get her brother-in-law away from that tree.

"Thomas wouldn't want you to fall apart," explained Dorcas. "Henry said that two of you were taking turns using Thomas's gun. It could have just as easily been him pulling the trigger and you behind the tree."

Robert sighed and laid his head back against the tree.

"I suppose so, but it wasn't me. It was him. It was Thomas."

"You can run that around in your head over and over again, but it won't change a thing, son. You just get up off that ground now and come be with your family," commanded Dorcas. "Sitting here is doing nobody any good at all."

"Come brother," said Arthur, standing in front of his brother and offering his hand.

Thomas took Arthur's hand and pulled himself onto his feet and away from the tree. Lucinda stood and put her arm around her husband's waist, while Henry put a guiding hand on his back. Dorcas wrapped a protective arm around Elizabeth and they made their way to Tom and Elizabeth's cabin. As soon as they walked out of sight, one of the soldiers walked down to the creek for bucket of water to wash the blood from beneath the tree. He knew it was best if the evidence of the tragedy was washed completely away as soon as possible.

Sarah, Jane, Margaret and Margery worked to get the tavern in shape for what they knew the next few days would bring, freeing Dorcas to stay by Elizabeth's side every waking moment. Thomas was to be laid out at the tavern and, after the preaching and the burying, the wake would be held there. They pushed the tables and chairs back, readying the space for the coffin. They checked the stores to see that there would be sufficient food and drink. While they worked, the undertaker was summoned and Arthur's officers worked together to build the table where Thomas would lay in repose.

Once again, the mourning clothes would come out of the chests, along with the bunting and black ribbon that they'd used far too often over the past few years. A light supper would be needed. No one would want to eat but they would all have to eat something to keep up their strength. Jane and Margery had learned from Dorcas how to take charge and handle these difficult situations, putting aside their own feelings so that they could do what must be done. Lucinda and Robert spent many private hours in their cabin with Robert staring into the fire while Lucinda read to him from the Bible in hopes that he would find some comfort in the words that she read.

By the time Thomas's body was brought in, the house and the family were ready. Like many settlers, the Buchanans had suffered through much tragedy and had grown adept at handling whatever came their way, no matter how shocking or painful it might be. They found great strength in simply being in the company of their loved ones.

"Momma, I need to talk to you about something," said Arthur when they at last had a moment away from the crowd.

"I know what it is that's weighing on your mind, son. You need to follow your orders and move your troops out of here right quick, don't you?"

"Mmm," he mumbled, looking embarrassed at having to mention it.

"But you don't want to do it until we lay Thomas to rest?" He looked at his feet and shook his head.

"And it would be the right thing to do. If you don't get your troops there in time, many more of our men and boys may die in battle simply because they're outnumbered. We'll bury Thomas tomorrow afternoon and then you go on and do what you need to do. We can't let any more men die because of our grief. Thomas was a solider, too. He'd understand that more than just about anyone."

"Thank you for being so understanding, Momma."

"Besides, it'll be easier for us women to grieve in private once most of the troops move on down the road and leave us in peace. I don't mean to sound ungrateful. We appreciate all they've done for us thus far and what they all will be doing for us in battle, but there's so many of them. It'll be quieter here when you lead most of them off. So, after everything is said and done tomorrow, you go on don't worry about us here. You'll serve this family better fighting against the British then you ever could sitting here and watching us cry."

"One other thing, Momma."

"Robert?"

"Yes, Robert. I don't think he should go this time. I don't think he should face that long march and try to fight after what happened yesterday. And he likely won't want to pull a trigger for a long while to come, unless he absolutely has to."

"Well, I don't know what to think there. I'm not sure that his mind would be on the fighting. He might be more likely to get hurt or killed just because he was distracted. And, as you said, he might be reluctant to shoot, even to protect himself."

"Then we agreed he should stay here this time?"

"Don't I get a say in my own fate," Robert asked as he walked into the room.

"We weren't sure you wanted a say just yet," answered Arthur, searching his brother's eyes for the truth.

"Well, I'm a grown man and I will have my say in matters that concern me. I'm going to ride and fight right alongside you, brother. I'll do it for Thomas. It's the best way that I can think of to honor him. Stop the British in his name. I will fight and I will do everything that I can to help win that battle for Thomas." Robert had found a way to stand and fight against his grief. His mother stood up and hugged him.

"That's my boy. I'm so proud of you, Robert." Arthur smiled warmly and clapped his brother on the shoulder, just as proud as their mother was of Robert's courage and determination. He knew that his brother was carrying an overwhelming burden over the accident, a burden that would have wrecked any other man.

Folks paying their respects came and went all evening and the entire next day. Every soldier in the encampment came to pay respects, lining up outside the door and waiting for hours. A handful of the men discreetly slipped away to dig the grave in the family plot not far from the house.

The camp started to fold up as the men packed their belongings and prepared to ride as soon as Thomas was properly buried. They took extra care to make sure they left the grounds as neat and tidy as possible and that everything would be in good order for the family. They didn't want to leave anything at all for Mrs. Buchanan to have to tend to in her darkest hour.

Late in the afternoon, at Dorcas's direction, Arthur announced that it was time to walk to the cemetery. Thomas was carried to his grave and a few prayers were said. Arthur's men finished the burial as he walked his mother, Thomas's widow and the rest of the family back to the house. As soon as everyone was settled, Dorcas pulled Arthur into the kitchen.

"Son, it's time for you to lead your men now. You go and do what you know you have to do."

"Yes, Ma'am," he answered. "Are you sure that you don't want me to post more men here at the house to protect you all?" He knew there were plenty of armed men staying nearby to keep an eye on things but he desperately wanted to do more to help his family in this unfathomable time of sorrow.

"Arthur Buchanan! Stop fussing and trying to coddle me."

Arthur chuckled softly.

"I guess I forgot who I was talking to. Is there anything you need me to do before we go?"

"Not one thing. Well, I guess that's not quite true. There is one thing I want: I want you and your brothers to all come back in one piece. Git now," she said dismissively, as she fought back tears. She started to turn and walk away but impulsively turned back to him, stood on her tiptoes and kissed her son on the cheek before walking back toward the serving room.

Arthur watched her walked away and marveled at his mother's strength. She'd just lost a third son but still she carried on with her head held high, her wisdom, courage and strength unwavering. He'd just lost his third brother and wasn't sure that he himself could endure much more without breaking. Arthur knew that her heart was breaking but she would do what it took to stay strong in the presence of her family. She would not indulge in more than a few tears in the sight of others. She would only allow herself to fall apart later, after everyone else had gone to bed and no one needed her strength and comfort.

Chapter Twenty-Three
1778

1778 was a chaotic year on the frontier. As the revolution wore on in the eastern regions, *The Bounding Elk* continued to serve as the Kishacoquillas Valley camp. The valley itself seemed immune from the skirmishes but battles were being fought all around the perimeter of the valley, well within marching distance.

Arthur's brothers, cousins, friends and neighbors fought valiantly beside him, relying on his steadfast leadership. In the springtime, the frontier suffered many a massacre, leaving Arthur and his troops precious little time to rest. He led his men to Sinking Valley and Bald Eagle, doing all that they could to defend the settlers who were under attack. Sometimes they got there in time and at other times, they'd arrive only to find whole families brutally murdered in their own homes.

Arthur took several men west over the mountains and 50 miles from the valley to help General Daniel Roberdeau build a new fort to protect the lead mine activities and the settlers in that area. All along the way there and all along the way back, they picked up survivors of vicious attacks and led them to find shelter. The dead were hastily buried where they fell.

The Buchanan family continued to welcome refugees from the frontier to the protection of Old Town. It wasn't the least bit unusual to see Arthur leading a dozen refugees to the tavern.

No Regulars or Indians dared march directly into Old Town because Arthur's men had turned the area around the creek into a formidable military camp, offering reliable protection that could not be found elsewhere for many miles around. If the refugees could make it to Old Town, they could expect to shelter and security there.

The tavern and the cabins were filled quickly and, once they were full, wagons were used for makeshift beds. When the wagons were full, more tents were put up. Things were so crowded that the men slept in shifts more for a comfortable sleeping space than for safety's sake.

The men fought as fiercely as their lack of muskets and ammunition would allow. Arthur wrote several letters to the Executive Council, pleading for rifles.

Old Town, Juniata, May 9th, 1778
Sir,

I this moment received by Rob Moor Express, a letter from Cap. Bell, stationed at Bauld Eagle, which informs me that Simon Vaugh, one of his company, was killed on the 8th instant, at the house of Jones Davis, upon Bald Eagle Creek. Rob Moor being set off Express to inform me of what had happened, who, as came through Penns Valley, stopped at the house of Jacob Stanford to feed his horse, where he found said Stanford killed. Likewise and seeing no persona bout the house, he immediately took and rode off. We likely to be in great distress, numbers of the inhabitants have died down here and more are on the way. I sent six men as spyes to The Kittanning, one of whom only returned, who says there fired up by 100 Indians and he only escaped. Sir, please send by Express to Lieutenant Carothers for a supply of ammunition and arms, rifles only will do, to enable

us to make a stand against these savage enemies. All the arms and ammunition I have sent up to the guard at Sinking Spring Valley and Bald Eagle.
I am, Sir, your humble servant,
Arthur Buchanan

Dorcas laid a plate of food in front of Arthur just as he finished the letter.

"Momma, help me with this letter," pleaded Arthur. He was desperate, writing letters day after day, begging for arms and ammunition from anyone who might be able to send them. He was determined that his voice would be heard and that his men would be properly armed. "You seem to be able to talk folks into doing what they ought to do even when they don't want to do it. These men aren't listening to my pleas. Maybe you can help me find the words that'll turn their hearts."

"Well now, let me see what you wrote. Don't' know if I can do any good but I'll certainly try." She sat down next to him to read.

Kishacoquillas, 11th May, 1778
Dear Sir,

I have this moment received intelligence by express from Major Mils, in Penn's Valley, that the Indians continue to murder men, women and children on our frontiers; last Friday, Jacob Stanford, his wife and daughter were inhumanly killed and scalped and his son, a lad of ten or eleven years of age, is yet missing. The express informs me that the savages ravage all parts of our frontiers in a very public manner. I need mention nothing to you of the Tories, as they meet with too much encouragement to cease from their barbarous practices. I don't mean to blame you, but rather myself and others, who do not put it out of their power to injure us, as fast as we catch them; my zeal for my country's interest would prompt me to this, which, if I can obtain, pray order me to draw my sword. All I want is to have justice done to all men, to have villains tried for their offences; but it is well known that this is not the case, for instance Shelly, and others I can tell you of when we meet. I shall insist on this no farther.

I expect that you will assist us with arms and ammunition, as I now stand in need of four hundred weight of powder and lead, equivalent, and likewise with one hundred good rifles, if possible. We are in a very distressful situation at present, but I expect you will consider our condition and do all in your power to aid us. I have taken the sentiments of my battalion and they are briefly these: If the lieutenants of the county will send us the assistance of a few men with arms and ammunition, we will march immediately into the Indian country and attack their towns, which will be the most effectual method of calling them from our frontiers. We also think it very necessary that commissaries be appoint to raise provision and pack

> *horses provided to convey it to the assistance of our little camp. As the safety of this state, from our savage enemy, in a great measure on our being able to stand our ground, it is hoped will meet with suitable encouragement all necessary assistance.*
>
> *The express will assist in bring over the arms and ammunition, if they are ready. I hope you will reward him for his trouble.*
>
> *I am, Sir, with all respect, your very humble servant,*
>
> *Arthur Buchanan.*

"I don't believe I'd change a word of what you wrote here. You told the story and told him what your troops need. If that doesn't convince him to do what's right, then nothing will."

"Thank you, Momma. I hope that you're right."

"You got your father's way with words, that's for sure. You don't really need my help with your letters."

"Oh, but I do, Momma. I need your help every day in so many ways. You keep this whole camp fed and running right. Every man in this camp needs your help in one way or another."

Arthur grew impatient and decided not to wait for a reply to any of the letters that he'd sent by Express. He believed that only a bold, face-to-face confrontation would do, so he gathered a company of six men to ride along with him to Lancaster and stand before the Supreme Council. Certain that he could convince the Council to give him what he needed, he insisted that they ride to Lancaster in three wagons to bring back the arsenal of guns and ammunition that he meant to bring home. When Arthur and his small band of men appeared before the Council, the men behind the desk could no longer coldly ignore his pleas. His certainty paid off and the small caravan returned to Old Town bearing 50 rifles, 50 muskets and ample ammunition for both.

"See, Arthur, I told you that you could convince them to do what was right in the end," exclaimed Dorcas as she surveyed the cache.

"Well my letters didn't convince them but standing right there in front of them seemed to shame them into doing what they should do. Funny how they ignored all those letters but managed to come up with the guns when we walked in that door and they were forced to look us in the eye."

"All that matters is that you have what your men need now. I'm proud of you for not giving up. Your father would probably have done much the same. You're so like him. I'd bet money that he's looking down on you from heaven, proud as can be of what you did."

Chapter Twenty-Four

1779

"Artie," called Dorcas. "After you finish you breakfast, I want you to take John and a couple of the girls to go pick some apples. Grab some baskets out of the pantry. I want you to bring back as many apples as you can."

Jane and Charles' children, Artie and Lizzie, had come to stay with Dorcas for protection from potential danger. Jane and Charles wanted to stay over in Bedford County and protect their home, as well as their crops, but when they heard rumors of a roving band of violent Indians in the vicinity, they decided that it would be better for their son and daughter to stay encamped with Dorcas for the time being. Dorcas was happy to have her grandchildren with her, no matter what the reason. She missed those years when her children were home and young enough to be tucked into their beds each night.

"You boys each take a musket along. Can't be too careful these days."

"Grandma, the apple trees aren't all that far from house."

"Don't backtalk me, young man. Just do as you're told," she reprimanded him lightly.

"Yes, 'um." Like his namesake grandfather, he was wise enough to know when not to argue.

Dorcas was more nervous than usual these days. A large band of Indians had been spotted in Kishacoquillas Valley just a few weeks before and Arthur was somewhat worried that even Old Town might not be unassailable anymore, no matter how many soldier tents sat at the center of town.

While the children were busy working in the orchard, and Dorcas was sitting before her butter churn in the yard, two somber men came riding into the camp, followed by a third man driving a wagon. Dorcas recognized the men but couldn't think of their names. The horseback riders dismounted, tied up their horses and walked slowly but deliberately toward Dorcas. The wagon driver stayed put, shifting awkwardly in his seat. When the men took off their hats and bowed their heads to avoid eye contact, a strong sense of foreboding washed over Dorcas. She'd seen that look in men's eyes too many times.

"Um, Mrs. Buchanan . . ." uttered the taller of the two men.

"Yes. What is it?"

"I . . . I'm afraid I have some bad news for you."

"Whatever it is, young man, just spit it out and get it over with," she replied stoically, taking a deep breath and standing up from her chair to face whatever was coming. The truth was that she was feeling anything but stoic. Her knees were trembling and her stomach was churning. Her three remaining children were now out of her control and out from under her protection. She was convinced, down deep in her heart, that something terrible had happened to one of them. She could feel it in her bones. The only question was which child it would be this time.

"It's . . . well, it's your daughter, Jane." Dorcas fell back down to her chair, her hand covering her heart as though to protect it from what was about to break it. "She and Mr. Magill, well, we found 'em this morning. Looked like they'd been attacked by Indians but we couldn't tell for sure. Mrs. Buchanan, I'm afraid they're both gone."

Dorcas whimpered. Her head was whirling. Her only daughter. The fourth child she'd lost in as few as a dozen years. That she was gone now seemed impossible. And what about young Artie and Lizzie? Dorcas was so relieved that they were with her, for they surely wouldn't be living if they'd been at home with their parents. But now they'd just lost their parents and she would have to tell them the tragic news. How could she speak when she couldn't breathe? She couldn't move. She couldn't think. She wasn't even sure that her heart could continue to beat.

She had no choice but to breathe. She had no choice but to move. Her heart must continue to beat. Dorcas had to rally for her grandchildren. Now she had to go tell Artie and Lizzie the worst news they would ever hear. She had to be the one to break their hearts. She also had to be the one to take care of them in their time of grief. She'd make sure that they were always well taken care of.

So much needed to be done. Jane and Charles would have to be brought home to be buried. Their home would have to be cleaned up and likely sold. The rest of the children's things would need to be fetched. There were a great many things that would have to be done and Dorcas was running out of the physical, emotional and spiritual strength needed to do them.

She'd lost so much, so many people that she loved, over the past few years. She was exhausted. She was tired of all this death. Tired of the fear. Tired of the daily struggles that had to be overcome to merely survive. They'd come to this country to build a better life for themselves than they might ever have had in Monaghan.

There were days when it felt like that better life that they dreamt of and worked so hard for was just within their reach. On other days, it felt like an impossible dream. This was one of those apparently impossible days. She wondered how she could even think about a better life when she was getting ready to bury her only daughter, along with her son-in-law. How could she carry on now that most of the children that she had born and raised were gone?

"Ma'am? Mrs. Buchanan?" She'd been so overwhelmed and lost in her own thoughts that she'd forgotten that the bearers of the awful news were still standing in front of her. She looked at them mutely.

"Um, Ma'am, we have their bodies in the wagon."

"Oh," came her grieved reply. "I'll get some men to . . ."

"No, no. You just sit. We'll take care of everything. Is Colonel Buchanan hereabouts?" She nodded and gestured toward Armstrong's cabin, where Arthur was meeting with the officers under his command.

"I'll go fetch him." He turned on his heal and walked off in the direction of the cabin that Dorcas had directed him to. Dorcas took a deep breath and turned to face the apple orchard where her two unsuspecting grandchildren were happily picking apples.

Chapter Twenty-Five

It was an unusually warm day in October when Dorcas decided to move a chair outdoors, behind the house, to do her mending in the bright sunlight. She was facing the afternoon sun with her back to the woods while she concentrated on her stitching. Normally, she wouldn't have been so careless as to put her back to the woods, but her mind had been so muddled since Jane and Charles were murdered that she'd unintentionally let her guard down once in a while.

Dorcas was engrossed in her work and thinking about the events of the past few weeks, when she suddenly sensed someone or something moving furtively up behind her. Holding her breath, she moved cautiously, gently laying her work on her lap and subtly sliding her hand to the gun leaning on her right thigh. Her heart beating hard, she turned slowly to her left, the direction where the slight rustling she'd heard had come from.

She expected to see a couple of Indians, or perhaps a Loyalist or two. She did not expect to see a large, grey wolf creeping up on her, mere feet away from where she sat, with a look in his dark eyes that seemed to indicate that he intended for Dorcas to be his next dinner.

In a flash, the musket was at her shoulder and she'd fired a round, hitting the intimidating animal square between the eyes. Only when the creature was lying motionless on the ground was Dorcas able come to grips with what had just happened.

Gunfire was an everyday occasion in the valley, thanks to men hunting and shooting mark. However, this gunshot came from behind the tavern, far too close to the house to be anything but another catastrophic situation. Family and customers alike came running from the tavern, guns drawn, ready for battle. Soldiers came running from tents and cabins to investigate the source of the unexpected shot, armed and ready to fight off any intruders who dared to invade Old Town.

The women gasped in astonishment and the men chuckled with relief when they rounded the back of the cabin to find Dorcas, one hand still on her gun, the other on her chest, trying to calm herself from the unexpected excitement of the afternoon.

"Oh, Dorkey, are you alright?" asked Margery.

"I'm alright. Really, I am. I was frightened near to death for a minute there, but I'm fine now that it's all over. Don't you all go worrying about me none."

"We'll take care of this, Dorcas. You go on inside and let the ladies take care of you a while," suggest one of the soldiers. "You've just had an awful fright and you'll need some taking care of till you get all settled down again."

"Thank you, Alexander. I wouldn't mind going inside for a few minutes. That old fella there kind of shook me up," she said, gesturing to the dead wolf.

Margaret brought her a little chunk of bread with butter and a big glass of Madeira to wash it down.

"Thank you, Margaret. Normally, I wouldn't drink Madeira this early in the afternoon, but I believe that I'll make an exception today."

The customers gathered around the long table where Dorcas sat and asked her to tell how she came to shoot the wolf. These days, Dorcas rarely sat and talked in the tavern during the daylight hours but everyone insisted that she sit and recuperate after her harrowing experience. She was enjoying the rare chance to sit and chat with her friends and neighbors.

Once Dorcas finished sharing her harrowing story, others around the table shared their own tales of animal attacks, Indian ambushes, kidnappings, near misses, barn fires and battles between the Continentals and the Red Coats. The colonies were in turmoil every moment of every day, so there was no shortage of dramatic stories to tell. Each and every loss was shared and each and every victory celebrated across the community.

"Did you all hear about Chief Logan," asked one of the soldiers.

"No, what about him," asked Robert.

"Killed by one of his own people," came the answer.

"What? One of his own people? Are you sure?"

"Well, the details are a little sketchy. Nobody knows for sure. Some folks are saying his own nephew murdered him."

"Ah that's a shame. Poor man had more than his share of troubles in the past four or five years. He never was the same after his family was all kilt."

"God rest his soul. Who could ever recover from something as awful as that," asked Dorcas. "He was as decent a man as I ever knew, except my Arthur. They were so much alike, Logan and

Arthur. They both loved people and treated everyone right. Both were whip smart, too. It's no wonder they were such good friends. Two peas in a pod they were."

"They were both good men, that's for sure. The world's a darker place without them in it," remarked Robert. The table fell silent, and everyone sat staring sadly into the bottoms of their glasses.

Chapter Twenty-Six

Dorcas was in the kitchen, peeling a large pile of potatoes, when Robert rushed in the back door. He was slightly out of breath and had all the marks of a man on a mission.

"Momma, where's Arthur?"

"I don't know. I haven't seen him a couple of hours. Did you check his place?"

"Yes."

"Up the hill at the shooting ground?"

"Yes. He's not there either and I need to find him right quick."

"What's the trouble today," she sighed. She was growing weary of unfortunate news arriving on nearly a daily basis.

"Patrick Holliday just rode into camp and said that Captain Boyd, his rangers and some other scouts were ambushed by some Indians over at Frankstown. Killed nearly all of them. Only half a dozen out of the whole party escaped and made it to Frankstown to tell the tale. I have to find Arthur and give him the news as soon as possible."

"Check the other cabins. He's here somewhere close by. I just saw Clones out in the barn, so I know he didn't ride off anywhere."

"I'm here," announced Arthur as he walked in the door. "Sam found me and told me what happened, and he gave me a letter from George Ashman explaining it all."

5th June, 1781

Sir, by an Express this moment from Frankstown we have the bad news. As a party of volunteers from Bedford was going to Frankstown, a party of Indians fell in with them this morning and killed thirty of them. Only seven made their escape to the garrison of Frankstown. I hope that you'll exert yourself in getting men to go up to the stone and pray let the river people know as they may turn out. I am in health.

Geo. Ashman

"What are you going to do," asked Dorcas.

"We can't run off and fight right just yet. We're running low on guns, lead and powder. Dangerously low. We couldn't hold our own for more than a day or so with what we have. I'm going to have Captain Kelly and a couple of his men take a letter to Captain Postlethwaite over in Carlisle. If we're going to keep up this fighting, we need considerably more arms and ammunition than we have."

> *June 8, 1781*
> *Captain Samuel Postlethwaite, Q.M.*
> *Carlisle*
> *Besides the above we have intelligence from Penns valley that the enemy is this day discovered at that post and don't know when they mean to attack our people. Col. Brown yesterday marched a party of men to the stone and this day Cap. Means with a party marches to Penns valley to reinforce that post. The last of the ammunition I gave out last night, which was about three loads a man and if there is not a supply of that article, our young men can't turn out to defend our country in time of danger. The bearer Mr. Matthew Kelly will inform you of the particulars. I should be very fond if you would send over to me 100*

weight of powder, 200 weight of lead and 100 flints. Your compliance will much oblige your friend.
Arthur Buchanan

"Do you think he'll send what you ask for," asked Dorcas.

"I don't know. I don't know if he even has that much to send or that he'll be good enough to send it even if he does have it. He knows that we are in dire need. I'm going to go find Matthew and have him head out as soon as possible."

Captain Matthew Kelly accepted his orders and hastily summoned three of his men to accompany him to Carlisle. He and his men returned a few days later, bearing only 60 pounds of lead, 40 pounds of gun powder and 100 flints, less than half of what Buchanan had requested.

"He said he gave me all he had to give," explained Matthew. "Claimed he gave me his last bit of all of it.

"It's not enough. If we're going to put up any kind of a fight at all, we need more," groused Arthur. "I'm going to have to appeal to someone besides Postlethwaite."

"Who, though?"

"George Steward. If there's any supplies to be had, he'll get me what I need - if it can be had at all. Are you up for another quick ride?"

"Of course, I am. I should get a fresh horse, though."

"You go saddle up my Clones while I write the letter. By the time you've got him ready to go, I'll have the letter ready."

> *June 17, 1781*
> *George Steward, S.L.C.C.*
> *D.M. Steward, yesterday receiving these accounts from our frontiers, besides divers reports from Standing Stone, our inhabitance is in great distress as their arms and ammunition is detained by those men that the arms were sent by. I expect that murder will be done every day in our inhabitance. I could wish that in your wisdom might do something in this matter excuse, haste all from your friend.*
> *Arthur Buchanan*

Young Captain Kelly was once again on the road to beg for the tools essential to the survival of their community and the valley. Upon hearing Buchanan's desperate plea for assistance, Steward immediately scrounged up what supplies that he could spare and had them loaded into Kelly's wagon. Seward's contribution, combined with the small cache that Postlethwaite had sent, would enable Arthur and his men to keep up a solid defense in the valley, at least for a time.

Even so, the valley's families found little solace in that knowledge. Every day was fraught with danger. They were constantly looking over their shoulders and searching the shadows of the forest for Indians from the west or Red Coats from the east. Merely surviving from one day to the next proved to be a continuous struggle. Most of the Kish Valley citizens felt as though the threats and violence might never end. Terror permeated every aspect of their lives.

The leaves slowly began to change color up and down valley, turning the hillsides into a patchwork quilt of orange, red and golden hues. A sudden glimmer of hope floated into Old Town along with the autumn leaves, when an Express rider rode up to the tavern. Among the parcels and correspondence in his pack, he carried with him a letter and a newspaper sent from Arthur's commander in the east. The Express rider delivered Arthur's package straight to his cabin before coming to the tavern, as was his practice when Arthur received mail from the east that appeared to be important. The rider was just sitting down to his lunch when Arthur came running out of his cabin.

"Huzzah," Arthur yelled. "Everyone come meet up in front of the main house. I've got great news to share. Go gather up everyone in town and come on now. I've got a big announcement to make."

The men who were standing with Arthur when he got the news ran out and rousted soldiers from their tents, the shooting grounds and the creek. They tore up and down the dirt streets of Old Town, stirring up the falling leaves, ringing bells, hollering over fences and knocking on doors until every soul within walking distance was summoned.

The sense of urgency was palpable. Men stopped working and left their plows right where they stood. Women left their laundry boiling over the fire and bread still sitting in their bake ovens. The impromptu gathering became the largest and the most important Carlisle had ever seen. When he was certain that the crowd had all gathered together, Arthur stood on a bench in the midst of them.

"Listen up now, all of you." Arthur held the newspaper up high in front of him and read aloud.

> *Be it remembered!*
> *That on the 17th Day of October, 1781, Lieut. Gen. Charles Earl Cornwallis, with above 5000 British troops, surrendered themselves prisoners of war to his Excellency Gen. George Washington, commander in chief of the allied forces of France and America.*
> *Laus Deo!*

"Huzzah! Huzzah! Huzzah!" The cheers echoed throughout the valley until Arthur raised his hand to silence the crowd.

"Listen now and I'll tell you more." The crowd eagerly obeyed, and all eyes fell on him.

"According to my command, Cornwallis thought he had our men outnumbered at Yorktown and that he would win the war. Our troops surprised him with their numbers and their determination, and he was forced to admit that they were defeated. Now, I have to tell you that there's still some fighting going on here and there, but we expect it will all be over soon. I think that it's not far wrong to say that we are going to win this war for our independence."

"Huzzah! Huzzah! Huzzah!"

With that, Arthur stepped down from his makeshift podium and joined the raucous celebration.

Once again, Dorcas found herself nailing newspapers to the front door of the tavern and on every available space inside. Old Town reverberated with a great sense of liberation.

Not long after the news of Cornwallis's defeat spread, new settlers rolled into the region from points east. Trees were felled, new cabins were built and new fields were plowed. For the first time in several years, folks felt free and able to make plans for the future.

"Did you all read that story about the surrender," asked one man of a dozen men sharing the big table in front of the fire.

"It was shameful. Cornwallis showed his true self," answered another. "Claiming to be too sick to show up. Sending General O'Hara to hand over his sword. Humph!"

"Ill, my foot," exclaimed Dorcas as she delivered heaping plates of food to the table.

"That man was just plain, old-fashioned embarrassed. Too proud to surrender."

"In my opinion, he showed himself to be a true coward."

"Brits always have been sore losers," declared the first man.

Chapter Twenty-Seven
1782

Even though the war was presumably over, or nearly so, the settlers' troubles weren't quite yet over. The Indian attacks continued for nearly two years after the surrender at Yorktown. At the beginning of the war, the British paid some tribes bounties for scalps and prisoners, and it took several months after British laid down their arms to convince them to stop the practice. During the peace negotiations, the Brits tried to restrain their former allies but the Indians would have none of it. Incensed that the British were giving up, the Indians instead increased the number of attacks and the militia fought back hard. Neither side showed the other side any mercy whatsoever.

On a cold damp afternoon, Dorcas draped a woolen shawl over her shoulders and stomped out the door of the tavern, in search of Arthur. He was standing before the hearth of his own cabin, talking to some of his men, when his mother threw open the door. All eyes turned to the tempest in the doorway.

"Arthur Buchanan, Jr., I want to talk to you right now," demanded Dorcas. The fire in her eyes and the set of her jaw let Arthur know in no uncertainty that his mother was as angry as he had ever seen her.

"Gentlemen, would you please excuse us so that my mother and I can chat for a while." The men wasted no time jumping from their chairs and rushing out the door, nearly falling over each other in their haste. They wanted no part of whatever it was that Dorcas was apparently about to unleash on her son. As soon as the door shut behind the last man out, Arthur pulled out a chair for his mother.

"Momma, sit down and tell me what in the world has you so riled up." He could tell that he was in for a thorough tongue-lashing from his powerhouse mother. He remained calm while he awaited the unleashing of her wrath.

"No, I will not sit down. I'm far too angry to sit."

"What has happened, Mother? I've never seen you so irate."

"I just heard tell of a bunch of militiamen murdering innocent Christian Indians over in Gnadenhutten. Nearly 100 of them. They were kilt while they were praying and singing. Then those vile men burned down the whole village. Shameful. It's just shameful beyond words."

"Yes, Ma'am. I heard about that disgraceful attack, and I feel the same way you do about it."

"Tell me you and your men had no part in that unforgivable mess," she demanded, tears filling her eyes. "Tell me. I didn't raise any of my sons to be murderous animals."

"Oh, good heavens! No, Momma. How could you ever think of such a thing? Not me nor any of my men had anything to do with it. I'd tan the hide of any one of my men who would do something like that. I do not kill innocent people, nor would I allow any of my men to. I heard tell it was a bunch of fellows from over around Pittsburg."

Dorcas sighed with relief and finally sank into the chair Arthur offered.

"You honestly didn't think that I'd have anything to do with that kind of thing, did you, Momma? Me or my men?" Hurt clouded his eyes.

"No, son. Not in my heart of hearts but I just had to make sure. No, I really do know better than that."

"You know that I've had to kill men during the war, but I promise you that I never did anything that I didn't absolutely have to do."

"I guess I know that but I had to find out for sure. That story makes my stomach churn. Innocent, peace-loving people murdered for no reason at all. Hearing about it made me so angry that I just couldn't see straight. I couldn't think straight."

"That story would make any decent human being feel the same way. Those men were horribly out of line. I heard they were militia, but the reality is that I believe they were rogue rebels masquerading as militia. No responsible Continental or militia leader would sanction that kind of attack, let alone lead it."

"I just can't imagine what kind of man would have any hand in that," she said.

"Nor can I."

A scant two months later, another story of innocents being murdered drifted into the tavern when Minerva Wallace came to trade.

"Good morning, Dorcas."

"Well, hello Minerva. I haven't seen you in much lately."

"I was laid up with the fever for a few days but I'm better now."

"Glad to see it. You have some butter there for me?"

"I do. Can I trade you some eggs for it?"

"Of course. Can you sit and stay a while?"

"Certainly. I've been shut up for long that I need to catch up with everything that's been going on around town."

"Let's go sit in my kitchen where no one will bother us." Minerva followed Dorcas to the cozy kitchen at the back of the house.

"Did you hear that Penelope is expecting," asked Minerva.

"No! How exciting that is. I know that she's wanted and waited for a child for a long, long time. She once told me that she didn't think that she could have a child. When is the baby to come?"

"In about four months, I think."

"It's good to have some happy news for a change."

"I some more happy news for you."

"Well now, for a woman who has been shut up, you seem to have a lot of news of your own."

"This news came direct to me in my sick bed. My son Jesse sent us a letter and said he's going marry that Reynolds girl that he's been courting over in Philadelphia. We'll be heading over there for a wedding in a few weeks."

"That is wonderful, Minerva. You must be awfully happy."

"I am. She comes from a very good family. It's a wonderful match."

"I have to tell you, it's refreshing to hear some good, old-fashioned woman talk. The only stories that men bring into the tavern is bad news. Seems to me that all they talk about is folks getting robbed, hurt or killed."

"Unfortunately, there is plenty of that kind of thing going on."

"Too much. And I suppose that we do need to know when and where it happens so that we know if trouble might be heading our way."

"Speaking of trouble, Dorkey, I hate to ask when we've been talking about happy things, but have you heard about any recent trouble anywhere close?"

"The biggest story going around right now is that the Corbly family was murdered near Garard's Fort. They were on their way to church on Sunday morning."

"The whole family?"

"Mr. Corbly and the oldest two children lived but the whole family was attacked."

"Indians?"

"Uh-huh. Reverend Corbly said they were walking to the church where he preached but he forgot his Bible and turned back to get it. They weren't far off, so Mrs. Corbly and the children just kept strolling towards the church. There hadn't been any trouble there for a long time, so they thought they were safe."

"Oh, my heavens. I'm not sure any place at all is completely safe these days. What happened then?"

"The Reverend said he thinks that some men in a hunting party were up on Indian Point and spied Mrs. Corbly and their five children walking with no man and no weapons. They worked their way down the hillside and attacked the family just before they reached the church."

"They attacked a lone mother and her children? What is this world coming to? Then what happened?"

"Reverend Corby told that just as he reached the last rise in the road, he heard his wife and children screaming. He ran to try to help them but an Indian came at him with a gun, and he had to turn away. They killed the baby in her arms, her little boy and another young daughter. The oldest two daughters ran and hid but the Indians found them later. They were scalped, but for some reason, the Indians didn't kill them."

"Poor Reverend Corbly, seeing his family killed like that. How terrible for them all."

"What angers me is that it's happening on both sides. I keep hearing stories of several white men being just as savage in their attacks on the tribes."

"I sometimes think these men just fight because they like to fight. What reason is there to kill harmless women and children?"

"I wonder about that every day."

True, lasting peace seemed a long way off, but peace was eventually born, after a long, slow labor. The attacks between the natives and the colonists abated month by month and finally trickled down to a scarce few. The peace negotiations that had begun in 1782, finally succeeded in September of 1783, when the Treaty of Paris was signed and the Revolution officially came to an end.

The following March, Colonel Buchanan received orders to disband his militia, allowing his men to return to their homes throughout the valley and surrounding towns. As the soldiers drifted away, old friends and neighbors who had fled to the protection of bigger cities during the war, ultimately came back to reclaim their homes. New settlers also came to the valley seeking whatever opportunities they might find there.

Sooner or later, old and new settlers alike wound up at *The Bounding Elk*, seeking like-minded souls for socializing and celebrating. They drank more than usual and ate more than usual. They stayed later than they would have dared in years past, toasting their successes and their future.

It was time to rebuild and strengthen Old Town and the surrounding area. Old Town blossomed and grew from being a small settlement to being a proper town with all the government and industry that one would find in any other burgeoning Pennsylvania town. The first official election was held at the tavern in October and over 600 men voted Mr. Frederick Watt as the town's first assemblyman.

Every meeting or event or any importance at all was hosted at *The Bounding Elk.* The dreams that Arthur and Dorcas shared when they built the place nearly 30 years ago, were realized each and every day. Dorcas never spoke a word to anyone about it but she often bemoaned the fact that her beloved Arthur couldn't be there to be a part of all the goings-on and excitement in the valley. He would have reveled at being at the heart and soul of it all.

Chapter Twenty-Eight
1788

"How you doing, Momma," asked Arthur. He and his mother had left Bedford County just before dawn and spent the past several hours bouncing around on the wooden wagon seat. He tried to avoid the deep ruts in the road as much as possible but it was tough going.

"Tolerable, but I don't mind saying that my backside is aching," she answered. "This bench seat gets feeling pretty hard after a few hours."

"It certainly does. It has been a long ride but it's not too much further, though. We should be home by sunset or not too long after."

"I should have brought a cushion along to sit on but my mind was on more important things than comfort. I'll be glad to get home. I'm awfully tired."

"I'm sure you are. We've had a few difficult days, haven't we?" They were on their way home from his eldest brother Henry's funeral in Huntingdon. The rest of the family had returned two days prior. Arthur and Dorcas had stayed a little longer to help his widow Sarah get things in order.

"It certainly has. One of the hardest times of my life - God knows I've seen my share of hard times." Dorcas sadly stared at the road ahead. "Sarah said he went peacefully, though. She said she was sleeping next to him, and he never cried out or anything. He just drifted away."

"When my time comes, I hope that's the way I go."

"That's the way I feel, son. You know, no mother should outlive her children and now I've lost all but you and Robert. I gave birth to seven and now I've buried five. I don't believe I could stand to bury another." Arthur longed to comfort his mother, but at this moment, he was at a complete loss for words. She'd always been such a strong woman but Henry's death had taken a toll on her soul.

"So many women I know have lost husbands and children. I am not alone in that unfortunate circumstance. I know that I was blessed to ever have such a big, wonderful family to begin with. Not everyone has had what we've had. Your father and you children have been the greatest blessings of my life."

"You have been our greatest blessing, Momma. We couldn't have asked for a better mother. And I couldn't have asked for better brothers or a better sister."

"I always appreciated the way that your papa treated Henry and Thomas, just like they were his own. And none of you ever treated them any different despite their having a different father."

"It never would have occurred to any of us to treat them any different. We grew up under the same roof with them. We worked together, fought together and stood by each other thick and thin. They were our true brothers, no matter what anyone else might think or say."

Dorcas smiled softly through her tears. Memories flashed before her eyes when she thought of all the years that they'd shared, especially since they'd come to Kish Valley. They'd gone through so much there alongside her beloved creek, both good times and bad.

They'd built a wonderful home and business. She'd watched her husband and sons chop down the logs and stack them to create their precious home. Then when the children came of age, they created their own small village when each one of the Holt and Buchanan children built homes within steps of each other. They stood unfailingly by each other during the bad times and the good.

In her mind's eye, Dorcas could see her daughter and daughters-in-law working together in the garden and the kitchen. She saw her husband, sons and son-in-law working as a team to build the cabins. She remembered the times when the children were young and she would take them on walks through the forest, foraging for nuts and berries. She recalled when they would gather around the fire at night and they would listen with rapt attention to Arthur's stories of Ireland and his family before him. They'd gone down on their knees as one to pray. They'd rejoiced when the war was over and even more when new babies came into the family. They'd danced with each other at weddings. They'd cried with one another at graves. Through it all, they stood steadfast, each one unfailingly devoted to the others.

Dorcas was exceptionally proud of every one of her children. They'd all grown up to be good, respectable people. They worked hard, built nice homes, raised families and helped others whenever the need arose. She hoped and prayed that all of her grandchildren would grow up to be just as hard-working, respectable and God-fearing as their parents had proved to be and there already was strong evidence that they would do just that.

She'd already seen some of the oldest ones grow up and do right by the family name but it grieved her that she likely wouldn't live long enough to see how the youngest ones turned out. She wanted to stay forever. She longed to take care of her family for as long as she could. She was quite aware, though, her time on earth was limited.

"We've certainly had a lot of happy times and a lot of exciting adventures, haven't we?"

"Yes, ma'am," he agreed. "And we have more happy times ahead of us, if it's not wrong to say so, so soon after burying Henry. We still have you, me, Sarah, Margery, Robert and Lucinda. And all those grandchildren and great-grandchildren of yours! This big, old Buchanan clan still has a bright future."

"It does, doesn't it?" The thought of the world being filled with her grandchildren and great-grandchild children, gave her an overwhelming sense of joy, whether she would be there to witness it or not.

"And speaking of the future, there's something I've been wanting to talk to you about. Now's as good a time as any, since we're out here alone this road and have plenty of time to talk. I hope you don't think it inappropriate to speak of it now when we're still in mourning."

"There's never an inappropriate time for a son to talk to his mother of something heavy on his mind and I can tell whatever it is, it is laying heavy on you."

"Then I'll just spit it out as frank as I can: I want to buy the tavern of you."

"Mmm," she murmured in agreement. "I have to agree. It's better that I sell it to you now rather than you and your brother having to deal with it after I'm gone. Remember how long it took to settle your father's estate? I don't want you boys to go through that when I pass on. If I sign it all over now, then I die owning nothing but my clothes. Besides, you've been running it mostly by yourself these days anyway."

"But you still rule the roost, Momma. I just do whatever it is that you tell me to do."

"No, I'm just advising you. You've been doing all the hard work. It's high time that I sign it over to you. You've earned it. You're as good a man as your father was and I trust you to keep it running right, just like he would have, for a long time to come."

"But don't you want to keep running it for a while longer?"

"Arthur, we just buried your brother. He looked healthy but died in his sleep at the age of 57. I'm 78 years old and slowing down. We both know that I could go at any time. I've already outlived a good many women that I've known all my life."

"Oh, Momma, please don't talk like that. I couldn't bear to lose you so soon."

"Well now, don't go getting all torn up about the idea. I might be around to pester you another 20 years or so. You know that the women in my family tend to live a long time, if they get to go naturally. "

"From your lips to God's ears!"

"You know, we need to make this right with Robert. Even things up to be fair about it."

"I was just thinking about that, too."

"I've been thinking on this long before you brought it up and I have an idea. I know that he's not interested in owning a part of the tavern. He has other things in mind for his future. Let's sit down and figure out about what the tavern and the land are worth, then divide it in two so that you get half and Robert gets half. I'll give you your half right out, then you pay me the other half of the value and we'll give that money to Robert. You both get your inheritance early – yours will be the tavern and his will be the money. He'll appreciate having the money to do whatever he wants to do. I know he's interested in some choice land down south of Carlisle."

"That's a good plan. And a fair one. But Momma, you'll still help me keep the tavern running, won't you?"

"Of course, I will. I'll have to earn my room and board, won't I?"

"After all you've done for me since the day I was born, you don't need to earn a thing. I owe you more than I could ever repay you. I sure do want your advice, though."

"You'll get my advice whether you want it or not."

"I have no doubt of it. I have no doubt whatsoever."

Two weeks later, Dorcas signed the tavern over to Arthur and 2000 pounds over to Robert. All three of them walked away completely satisfied with the arrangement. After their business was concluded, the two brothers strolled down to the creek to enjoy some fishing.

"Are you sure that you're alright with this arrangement, Robert," Arthur asked as soon as they were out of earshot of the tavern.

"Of course, I am. Why would you ask?"

"Because this place isn't just a business. It's our family homestead."

"I am still welcome to come visit from time-to-time, aren't I," he joked.

"We'll have to see about that," Arthur quipped. "But in all seriousness, I want you to know that if you ever change your mind and want be a part of it, you're always welcome to come back and join me in running the place."

"I appreciate that, brother. I honestly do. Meantime, I am content that we are leaving it in your capable hands. I'm sure you'll carry things on just as our folks always did. I suspect that the Buchanan legacy will carry on strong for many years to come."

Epilogue

Dorcas Armstrong Holt Buchanan died at her home in Lewistown, Pennsylvania on February 22, 1804. She left behind 118 living descendants. Her grave can be found in the Lewistown Town Cemetery, just a few yards away from where *The Bounding Elk* once sat.

Strangers erected her tombstone in 1835. Two young men who had heard the myriad of stories about Dorcas were appalled that her grave, though well-known, was not marked with a more permanent remembrance. They went up to Shade Mountain, found a large stone and carved her name and date of death on it, then lugged it, along with a smaller stone, back to the cemetery. The larger piece was carved with her name (misspelled as Darcus) and placed at the head of her grave, while the smaller one was set at the foot of her grave.

Arthur and Robert were the only of Dorcas's children to survive her. They both later died in Lewistown and are buried near Dorcas.

It is unknown how many of their descendants are living today but that number surely must be in the thousands.

The Obituary of Dorcas Armstrong Holt Buchanan

This obituary was printed in *The Western Star* (Lewistown), *circa* 1804:

> *Departed this life in the vicinity of Lewistown, Feb. 22, 1804, Mrs. Dorcas Buchanan, at a very advanced age. She was born in 1712 and was therefore 93 years of age. Native of the county of Monaghan, Ireland, and emigrated with her parents and husband to Pennsylvania when a young woman and settled on the spot where Carlisle now stands. She resided there until 1753 at which time, with her husband and family, she removed to the banks of the Juniata, settling at the mouth of Kishacoquillas Creek, being the first white woman to pass through the Long Narrows. They lived in the midst of the Shawnee and Delaware tribes of Indians, who at that time owned*

the country now comprising Mifflin County. She became very friendly with the Indians and learned to speak their language. She was always warned when danger threatened. She was first obliged to flee at the time of Braddock's War, and had removed as far down as where Patterson's Mills now stand, above five miles below Mifflintown. A body of savages were descending the Juniata, they had plundered the dwelling of several white families who lived along its banks. They stopped opposite the temporary home of Mrs. Buchanan. She immediately demanded the property of the white people, and without waiting for an answer, began to secure it. The savages surrendered. She lost her sight at the age of 55 years and recovered it 23 years later. Logan, the great chief, was very intimate with Mrs. Buchanan and her family. Her progeny was numerous –

numbering in all 118 children, grandchildren, great-grandchildren and great-great grandchildren. One son was Colonel Arthur Buchanan.

Children and Grandchildren of Dorcus Armstrong Holt Buchanan

Henry Holt
    Wife: Sarah
    Daughter: Sarah Holt

Thomas Holt
    Wife: Elizabeth Mitchell
    Son: John Holt
    Son: William Holt
    Son: Thomas Holt, Jr.
    Daughter: Elizabeth Holt
    Daughter: Mary Holt
    Daughter: Dorcas Elizabeth Holt
    Daughter: Eleanor Holt
    Son: James Holt

Armstrong Buchanan
    No spouse and no children on record

William Buchanan
    Wife: Margaret Lycons
    Son: Arthur Buchanan
    Son: John Buchanan

Arthur Buchanan, Jr.

Wife: Margery
Daughter: Mary Buchanan
Son: Armstrong Buchanan
Daughter: Jane Buchanan
Son: Gregg Buchanan

Jane Buchanan
Husband: Charles Magill
Son: Arthur Magill
Daughter: Elizabeth Magill

Robert Buchanan
Wife: Lucinda Landrum
Daughter: Dorcas E. Buchanan

Bibliography

Ancestry.com

History of the Early Settlement of the Juniata Valley, U.J. Jones, Outlook Verlag, 1856

It Happened in Mifflin County, American History with a Central Pennsylvania Connection, Forest K. Fisher, The Mifflin County Historical Society, 2004

Juniata, River of Sorrows, Dennis P. McIlnay, Live Oaks Press, 2003

Mifflin County, Pennsylvania in the Revolution, 1775-1783, Raymond Martin Bell, 1993

The Descendants of Dorcas Armstrong Holt Buchanan: Pioneer Woman of Lewistown, Pennsylvania : with a Note on Andrew Lycans, Raymond Martin Bell, R.M. Bell, 1954

The Genesis of Mifflin County Pennsylvania, John Martin Stroup and Raymond Martin Bell, Mifflin County Historical Society, 1957

Made in United States
North Haven, CT
05 February 2024